Annie O'Neil spent most of her childhood with her leg draped over the family rocking chair and a book in her hand. Novels, baking, and writing too much teenage angst poetry ate up most of her youth. Now Annie splits her time between corralling her husband into helping her with their cows, baking, reading, barrel racing (not really!) and spending some very happy hours at her computer, writing.

MAKING CHRISTMAS SPECIAL AGAIN

ANNIE O'NEIL

MILLS & BOON

First published in Great Britain 2019
by Mills & Boon, an imprint of HarperCollins*Publishers*
1 London Bridge Street, London, SE1 9GF

Large Print edition 2020

© 2019 Annie O'Neil

ISBN: 978-0-263-08562-4

MIX
Paper from
responsible sources
FSC www.fsc.org FSC C007454

This book is produced from independently certified
FSC™ paper to ensure responsible forest management. For
more information visit www.harpercollins.co.uk/green.

Printed and bound in Great Britain
by CPI Group (UK) Ltd, Croydon, CR0 4YY

This one goes out to my ladies who create! Thank you so much Annie C, Karin and Susan for, once again, being epically fabulous. xx

CHAPTER ONE

HELL'S TEETH, IT was cold.

For once the all-consuming distraction of lungs vs arctic winds hurtling in from the Highlands was welcome. Physical pain outweighed Max Kirkpatrick's rage just long enough to remember that for every problem there was a solution. This time, though...

Trust the festive season to send him another blunt reminder that, no matter how hard he tried, the universe simply wasn't going to let him put some good back into the world.

He'd genuinely thought he'd done it this time. He really had.

His eyes travelled the length of the scrubby inner-city hospital then scanned the former vacant plot. There'd been snow on and off for weeks and yet there were still patients wandering around with pets and still more in the greenhouse, fostering their plants as if they were their own flesh and blood.

He traced his finger along a frost-singed rose. The parents of a little boy who'd lost his struggle with cancer had planted it three years earlier when Max had only just started Plants to Paws. The lad had loved coming out here to play with the family mongrel. Golden moments, his parents had called them. Golden moments. They still came and tended it as if their son were still with them. In a way, he supposed, he was.

This week.

Max's disbelief that someone was going to destroy the garden shunted through him afresh. Gone were the piles of rubbish, the burnt-out car, the thick layers of tagging on the side of the Clydebank Hospital walls. In their place were raised vegetable patches, benches with the names of loved ones on shining brass plaques dappled about the small wildflower meadow and, of course, the greenhouse and extra-large garden shed he'd built with a handful of other doctors. They'd recently installed a wood stove for added comfort. That would go, too. Along with the bow-laden wreath someone had hung on the door, despite his protestations that it was too early.

He crouched down to pop a couple of stones back onto the rock garden one of the Clyde's long-term leukaemia patients had helped build. Her first ever garden, she'd crowed. She'd be gutted when she found out it was going to be demolished, all to help some fat-cat property developer.

As he nestled another rock back into place, a young Border collie ran up to him with the tell-tale wriggle of a happy dog. She rolled onto her back for a tummy rub. He took a quick glance around and couldn't place her with anyone within sight.

He gave her soft white belly a rub. 'Hey, there, little one. You're a pretty girl. Now, who do you belong to?'

'Some would say they don't *belong* to any-one.'

The female voice slipped down his spine like warm honey. Low and husky, it was the type of voice that could talk a man into any-thing if he didn't watch himself. Good job he'd put the emotional armour on years back.

Max was about to say he was very familiar with the way canine-human relationships worked, thank you very much, when a pair of very expensive boots appeared on the woodchip path. Expensive boots attached to a public school accent. Still Scottish, but he would put money on the fact their schools had had a mixer dance. The military school his stepfather had deposited him in strongly encouraged shoulder rubbing with the 'power makers', as the school head had liked to call them.

'Deal breakers' would've been a better moniker if today's news was anything to go by. He still couldn't wrap his head round the hospital reneging on their word. Sure, they needed the money, but obliterating Plants to Paws to let a developer build a car park?

Bam! There went three years of hard work. Not to mention the slice of peace that came from knowing he'd finally made good on a years' old vow to do what he hadn't done for his mother: offer a refuge from a life that wasn't as kind as it should have been. All for a bit of money they'd never see on the wards. Hello, cement trucks, sayonara Plants to Paws.

The puppy nuzzled against his hand.

'What's her name?' He had yet to look up.

'Skye,' the voice said.

She sounded like a Christmas ornament. Angel? Whatever. Too damned nice was what she sounded.

Her leather boots moved in a bit closer. Italian? They looked handmade.

'I think you'll find her "love me tender" routine is an act. Skye's always got an ulterior motive and, from the look of things, you're playing right into her paws.'

He didn't even want to know what that meant.

'Is she a working collie or one of those therapy dogs?' They'd been trying to introduce the therapy dogs into the hospital but, as ever, stretched resources meant the lovable fur balls weren't seen much on the wards.

'Working. Though she's still in training. Precocious. Just like her mother.'

Damn. This woman's voice was like butter. Better. Butter and honey mixed together. If he was to add a shot of whisky and heat it up it'd be the perfect drink on a day like this.

'What type of training?' he asked, to stop his brain from going places it shouldn't.

'Search and rescue.'

That got his attention. He had been expecting agility. Maybe sheep herding. A voice like that usually came attached to some land. Land managed by someone else. As he tilted his head up, the sun got in his eyes and all he could make out was a halo of blonde hair atop a stretch of legs and a cashmere winter coat that definitely wasn't from the kind of stores he shopped in.

Miss Boots squatted down to his level and the second their eyes met he stood straight back up.

Piercing blue eyes. A tousle of short curls the colour of summer wheat. A face so beautiful it looked as though it had been sculpted out of marble. For every bit of wrong she elicited in his gut, there was an equal measure of good.

'Are you a patient?' It was the only thing he could think to ask, though he knew the answer would be—

'No.' She put her leather-gloved hand out to shake his. 'Esme Ross-Wylde.'

He kept his facial features on their usual setting: neutral. Though society papers weren't his thing, even *he'd* heard of the Ross-Wyldes. Scottish landed gentry of the highest order. The Ross-Wylde estate came with about five thousand acres, if memory served. A couple of hours north of Glasgow. Before his mum had married The Dictator, as Max liked to think of his stepfather, she'd taken him there for one of their famous Christmas carnivals. Huge old house. A castle actually. Expansive grounds. Extensive stables. Skating rink. Toffee apples and gingerbread men. It'd been the last Christmas he hadn't been made to 'earn his keep'.

'So.' He clapped his hands together and looked around the sparsely populated garden. 'Have you brought Skye along to meet someone?'

She unleashed a smile that could've easily lit him up from the inside out. Good thing she'd met him on a bad day. On a good one? He might have had to break some rules.

'I was looking for you.' She held up a familiar-looking scarf.

'How'd you get that?' He knew he sounded

terse, but with his luck she was the developer. If she was trying to sprinkle some sugar in advance of telling him when the wrecking ball would swing, she may as well get on with it.

Esme was unfazed by his cranky response. She tipped her head towards the garden shed as she handed him his scarf. 'A member of your fan club gave me this to give Skye a go at "search".'

He glanced over at the shed and, sure enough, there were a couple of patients from the oncology ward waving at him. Cheeky so-and-sos. They'd been trying to blow some oxygen onto the all but dead embers of his social life ever since they'd found out the nurses not so discreetly called him The Monk. He rolled his eyes and returned his attention to Esme Ross-Wylde. 'I presume that means you're here for the "rescue" part?'

She shrugged nonchalantly. 'If you're interested.'

Skye's tail started waving double time.

If he wasn't mistaken, the corners of her rather inviting lips were twitching with the hint of a smile.

Something about this whole scenario felt like flirting. He didn't do flirting. He did A and E medicine in Glasgow's most financially deprived hospital. Then he slept, woke up and did it all over again. Sometimes he came out here and dug over a veg patch. There definitely wasn't time for flirting.

When he said nothing she asked, 'How do you fancy keeping Plants to Paws the way it is?'

His eyes snapped to hers, and something flashed hard and bright in his chest that had nothing to do with gratitude. It ricocheted straight past his belt buckle and all the way up again. By the look on her face, she was feeling exactly the same thing he was. An unwelcome animal attraction.

Oh, hell. If life had taught him anything, it was the old adage that if something seemed too good to be true, it usually was.

The Dictator had taught him that everything came with a price. Best to rip off the plaster and get it over with. 'What's the catch?'

'Charming.' Esme quirked a brow. 'Is this how you win all the girls over?'

'It works for some.' Dr Kirkpatrick's shrug was flippantly sexy.

'Not this girl.' Her hip jutted out as if to emphasise the point she really shouldn't be making. That she fancied him something rotten and her body was most definitely flirting without her permission.

'Suit yourself.' His full lips twitched into a frown. Something told her it was for the same reason her mouth followed suit. They'd both been burnt somewhere along the line and if she was right, those burns had been slow to heal. If at all.

She sniffed to communicate she would suit herself, thank you very much, but the butterflies in her belly and the glint in his eye told her Max Kirkpatrick knew the ball was very much in his court.

He wasn't at all what she'd expected when she'd heard about an A and E doctor who'd set up a multi-purpose garden where patients could grow carrots and play with their pets. For some reason she thought he'd be older. Like…granddad old. And not half as sexy as the man arcing rather dubious eyebrows at her.

She called Skye to her and gave her head a little scrub. Here was someone she could rely on. Even as puppies, dogs were completely honest. Constant. Loyal.

Men? Not so much. Something she'd learned the hard way after her entire life had been splashed across the tabloids as a naive twenty-year-old who'd been taken for a fool. These days the Esme Ross-Wylde people met was friendly, businesslike and, despite the inevitable tabloid update on her charitable activities, able to keep her private life exactly that. Private. Which was a good thing because the rate of knots at which she was mentally undressing him would've won a gold medal.

'Are you going to tell me what the catch is or are you going to make me beg for it?' His frown deepened. As if he was fighting exactly the same onslaught of images she was. Sexy ones that most definitely shouldn't be drowning out any form of common sense.

Normally sponsoring a struggling charity was incredibly straightforward.

Normally she didn't feel as though her entire body was being lit up like a Christmas tree. Flickering and shimmering in a way she hadn't thought possible after years of protecting her broken heart. All of which was tying her insides in knots because feeling like a lusty teenager was not a safe way to feel. And yet…she couldn't tear her eyes away.

C'mon, Esme. You know the drill. Find a charity. Offer a lifeline in the form of a Christmas ball. Donate a couple of service dogs after two weeks of training up at Heatherglen. Job done.

She forced herself to answer. 'From what I hear, you might need my help.'

The doctor crossed his arms and squared his six-foot-something form so that she could see nothing else but him. Classic macho male pose. Designed to intimidate.

Although…she wasn't really getting that vibe from Dr Kirkpatrick. It was more protective than aggressive. There was something about the ramrod-straight set of his spine that suggested he'd done some time in the forces. Her brother had had the same solid presence. Unlike everyone else, who was bundled up to the eyeballs, Max Kirkpatrick wore a light fleece top bearing the hospital logo over a set of navy scrubs and nothing else. A normal human would've been freezing.

A normal human wouldn't be messing with her no-men-for-Esme rule. This guy? Mmm… Dark chestnut-brown hair. A bit curly and wild. The type that was begging her fingers to scruff it up a bit more. Espresso brown eyes. The fathomless variety that gleamed with hints of gold when the sun caught them. Everything about him screamed tall, dark and mysterious. And she liked a mystery.

No!

She did not like mysteries. She liked steady and reliable. Although…steady and reliable hadn't really floated her boat the last few times her brother had presented her with 'suitable dating material'.

Dr Kirkpatrick broke the silence first. 'Any chance you're going to explain this rather timely offer to rescue me?'

Ah. She'd forgotten that part. An oversight she was going to blame on Skye for unearthing the softer side of this impenetrable mountain of man gloom towering over her. Sometimes being short was a real pain.

'I run the Heatherglen Foundation. I founded it after my brother—an army man—and his service dog were killed in a conflict zone.'

A muscle twitched in his jaw. She'd definitely been right about the military.

She continued with more confidence, 'I am particularly interested in helping charities that use animals as therapy and who, more to the point, are in danger of closing. It's relatively straightforward. I select the charity, and in a few weeks the foundation will be hosting a Christmas ball, where the bulk of the funds raised will be donated to said charity, and ongoing support from the Heatherglen Foundation will also be provided.'

'Sounds great. Have a good time!' Max said in a 'count me out' tone.

'But—it'll save Plants to Paws.' Didn't he want his charity to survive? 'The ball's just before Christmas. It truly is a magical event.'

He rolled his eyes. 'So…what? Is this your stab at being Scotland's very own Mrs Claus?'

'There's no need to be narky about it. I'm trying to help.' She didn't like Christmastime either. Her brother had been killed on Christmas Eve and ever since then her favourite time of year had been shrouded in painful memories, but it didn't mean she took it out on others. Quite the opposite, in fact. The Christmas ball was her attempt to recapture the love she had for the festive season. Ten years and counting and it still had yet to take.

He opened his hands out wide. 'How would you feel if the one thing you'd poured three years of hard graft into was going to be paved over for a pay by the minute car park? At *Christmas*.'

'I'd do everything in my power to save it.'

'Trust a stranger I've never met to save a charity she'll most likely never make use of? I don't think so.'

She was hardly going to tell him to search the internet because, depending on which site he hit, he could definitely get the wrong impression. She took a deep breath and started over. 'The donors are personally selected by me. People who believe in giving back to

communities that have treated them well.'
The look he threw her spoke volumes. He
wasn't biting. She spluttered, 'Think of it as
your first Christmas present.'

'I don't trust things that come in pretty
wrapping.'

The way he looked at her made it crystal
clear he wasn't talking about ribbons and
sparkly paper. He was talking about her.

Now, *that* was irritating.

She wasn't some little airhead who bol-
stered her ego by doing seasonal acts of charity.

He shoved up his sleeve to check his watch.
'I've got patients to see and bad news to dispense, so if you don't mind…?'

'I *do*, actually. I mind very much.'

He rolled his finger with a 'get on with it'
spin.

What was with the attitude? Founders who
believed in their charities tended to drop it.
Not this guy. Either he'd been royally screwed
around at some point or was just plain old
chippy. Even worse, somehow, in a handful
of seconds, Max Kirkpatrick had slipped di-
rectly under her thick winter coat, beneath

her cashmere sweater and burrowed right under her skin, making this interaction feel shockingly personal.

The Heatherglen Foundation wasn't a platform for her to prance about Scotland, giving away her family's money. It was the one good thing that had come out of the most painful chapters in her life. As quickly as she'd been unnerved by his attitude, she'd had enough. She wasn't going to beg this man to take her money. He didn't want it? He couldn't have it.

She wiped her hands together as if ridding them of something distasteful. 'I came here with a genuine offer of help and a list of donors as long as my arm. If you're not interested in stopping Gavin Henshall from paving Plants to Paws over, I'll be on my way.'

He blinked. Twice.

Ooh. Had she found a chink in the strong, silent man's armour?

'I suspect it'll take more than a few thousand to keep Henshall at bay.'

He was right. She told him how much the last charity she'd sponsored had received.

He blinked again. 'Can we skip straight to

the what do I need to do to get the money part?'

Blunt. But it was a damn sight better than being dismissed as a bit of society fluff.

Her frown must've deepened because he suddenly folded into a courtly bow before unleashing an unexpectedly lavish charm offensive. 'I do humbly ask your forgiveness. Etiquette school clearly failed me. I didn't mean to be rude, Miss Ross-Wylde. Or is it Mrs?'

'Ms,' Esme snipped.

His eyes narrowed. Probably the same way hers had when he'd stiffened at the mention of Gavin Henshall.

He'd found her chink. She'd found his. Normally this would be her cue to run for the hills. But something about him made her want to know what made him tick. *Sugar.* Why couldn't Max Kirkpatrick have looked like a troll or been long since married to his childhood sweetheart? She checked his ring finger.

Empty.

Her heart soared so fast she barely knew what to do with herself.

Explain the details. Accept his refusal—because he will *refuse—then leave. Problem solved.*

She crossed her arms, aiming for nonchalant, not entirely sure if she'd hit her mark. 'I've just been up to speak to the hospital administrator, who has agreed to stall the sale until the new year. If the Christmas ball goes to plan, the hospital is happy to leave Plants to Paws as is.'

'In perpetuity?' Max obviously had his own set of conditions.

'Precisely. The only thing—'

He huffed out a laugh. 'I knew there was a catch.'

She let her eyebrows take the same haughty position his had earlier. 'The only thing, Dr Kirkpatrick, is that I require the head of each charity to select two patients whom you think might benefit from a service dog.'

'Oh. You require it, do you?'

She ignored him and soldiered on. 'We can offer the patient two weeks of one-to-one training at the canine therapy centre, all expenses included, and a follow-up care package if they have financial difficulties.'

His expression didn't change, but she could see he was actively considering her offer.

'What sorts of things do your dogs do, apart from search and rescue?' Max asked.

She smiled. She might have trouble bragging about herself, but she could big up her dogs until the cows came home. 'We have service dogs specially trained to work with epileptics, diabetics, people with cancer, people with mobility problems. I imagine you see the full gamut of patients in A and E. I'll forward you a full list of the services we can provide. We also have emotional support dogs, who work with people suffering from PTSD or anxiety.'

He nodded. 'Would I have to play any part in this?'

Normally he would, but no way was she inviting Max Kirkpatrick to Heatherglen. He was setting off way too many alarm bells. Before guilt could set in, she reminded herself that she made the rules. She could also bend them.

'Apart from attend the ball to receive a big fat cheque?' She shook her head. 'Not necessary. We're an all bells and whistles facility, so...' The lie came a bit too easily. She always invited the charity founder to join the patients and their families up at Heatherglen, but two weeks in close proximity with Max Kirkpatrick at this time of year, when the castle was romantically bedecked for the festive season? Not. Going. To. Happen.

Her mouth continued talking while her brain scrambled to catch up. 'We run the training sessions at our canine therapy training centre. There's also a medical rehabilitation clinic my brother runs in the main building. I have a week-long slot from December fifteenth up until the twenty-third of December, when we hold the ball. I understand the timing could be awkward with Christmas and family obligations, but as the developer is so keen to get construction under way, I thought we'd best get cracking. The patients could take the dogs home over the holidays then return for a second week of training sometime in January. If that suits.'

She watched his face go through a rapid-fire range of emotions. All of which he erased before she could nail any of them down.

'I'm fine with that,' he said evenly. 'As long as we make a few of my guidelines clear.'

Esme couldn't help it. She laughed. 'Excuse me, Dr Kirkpatrick. If I'm not mistaken, I'm the one helping you here and as such—'

'As such,' he cut in, 'I don't want you steamrolling my charity into something it isn't.'

'And what makes you think I plan on doing that?'

'Bitter experience.'

The second the words were out of his mouth Max regretted them. Hearing Gavin Henshall's name had a way of catapulting him straight back into the scrawny fourteen-year-old kid who'd mown lawns, taken out rubbish and thrown himself at all the rest of the chores his stepfather had set him as if his life had depended on it, only to discover he'd changed the goalposts. Again.

Military academy, apprenticeships over the summer holidays, boot camp. No matter what he'd done or how hard he'd worked, he had never been permitted into the house to shield his mum from the emotionally abusive relationship she'd unwittingly married into.

Not that he blamed her. They'd both fallen for Gavin's smooth lines. He'd promised her love, respect, a house with a big garden on the right side of town. A proper education for her 'shockingly bright boy', the son he'd always hoped to have.

How the hell Gavin had convincingly passed off the lies still astounded him. The only plus side of the cancer that had taken his mother's life was that it had freed her, at long last, from Gavin. It was more than he'd been able to do.

He shook his head and forced himself to focus on the here and now.

Esme Ross-Wylde didn't strike him as a steamroller socialite. The type of do-gooder who blithely floated round the city flinging gold coins for the 'have nots' to do her bidding. Sour memories teased at his throat. Money brought power and no one had made that clearer to him than Gavin. *'You earn your keep? You're in. You don't? You'll have to learn how to make a real man of yourself.'*

'What's your role in all of this?' Max had already been hit by one bombshell today. This one—the Henshall H-bomb—was making it harder to harness any charm. If he was going to tell everyone who cared about Plants to Paws it was going to survive, he needed to trust it was a genuine offer. Trusting a woman who could clearly cut and run from any scenario that didn't suit her was a tall order.

'Apart from being Mrs Claus, you mean?' She pursed her lips in a way that suggested he'd definitely hit a sore spot then said, 'As well as running the foundation, I'm a vet and an animal behaviour specialist. I also pick up poo, in case that's what you're really asking.'

It was all he could do not to laugh. Brilliant. Esme Double-Barrelled-Fancy-Boots picked up poo. It was a skilful way to tell him there was a vital, active brain behind the porcelain doll good looks. A woman who wanted to be mistress of her own destiny as much as he'd worked to be master of his.

'That it?' He knew he was winding her up, but…his flirting skills were rusty. Rusted and covered in a thick layer of dust if he was being honest.

Her smile came naturally, clearly more relaxed when talking about her work. 'The vet clinic is the only one in our area and the therapy centre's busy pretty much round the clock. The service dogs are trained to aid patients with specific tasks they are unable to do themselves. Like press an alert button for someone having an epileptic seizure, for example. Much like a dog who works on a bomb squad or for drug detection, they are not for the general public to cuddle and coo over.'

'That's the therapy dog's job?' Max liked hearing the pride in her voice as she explained.

'A therapy dog's main role is to relieve stress and, hopefully, bring joy—but often on a bigger scale. Retirement homes, hospital wards, disaster areas. An emotional support dog tends to provide companionship and stress relief for an individual. People with autism, anyone suffering from PTSD. Social anxiety. That sort of thing.'

Max nodded. The smiles on the faces of patients when they were reunited with their pets out here in the garden spoke volumes. Pets brought joy. Too bad people couldn't be counted on to do the same.

She continued, 'We're obviously highly selective, but find that dogs who come from animal rescue centres are particularly good for emotional support, learning and PTSD. The bigger dogs are wonderful with ex-soldiers who might need a service and emotional support dog all in one big furry package.'

He gave a brisk nod at that one. A few guys from his platoon could probably do with a four-legged friend. He still didn't know how he'd managed four tours in the Middle East without as much as a scratch. Physically, anyway. Emotionally? That was a whole mess he'd probably never untangle. 'And your brother? The one with the medical clinic?' Max crossed his arms again. 'How much of a say does he have in who I choose?'

A flicker of amusement lit up her blue eyes. One that said, *You think I let my big brother push me around?*

'My brother's a neurologist, but his clinic is predominantly for rehabilitation. The foundation has pretty much always been my baby, so…' There was a flicker of something he couldn't identify as she paused for breath. Something she was leaving out. When she noticed him watching her she quickly continued, 'You'll see for yourself when you come up to Heatherglen—' She stopped herself short.

'I was under the impression I wasn't invited.' He wasn't hurt by it. Had been relieved, in fact, but…he had to admit he was curious. And he wasn't thinking about the castle.

Her cheeks were shot through with streaks of red. 'Normally the head of the charity comes up, but I just assumed with the dates I have available being so close to Christmas… I just— I didn't think it would be feasible for you to come along and observe, so…' The rest of the sentence, if there had been any, died on her lips.

Max pulled up the zip on his fleece and glanced across at the hospital where an ambulance was pulling in. His break was coming to an end and this was already getting more complicated than it should be. No point in watching the poor woman squirm. She obviously had a big heart and he shouldn't play hard to get. The future of Plants to Paws was on the line. 'Don't worry about it. My dance card's been full for a while.'

'I see.' She tucked a stray curl behind her ear.

Max's thumb involuntarily skidded across his fingertips wondering if her hair felt as soft as it looked. He forced his voice into fact-finding mode. 'So where would the patients stay? If we go ahead with this.'

'At Heatherglen.' Esme reluctantly met his eye. 'The castle has been partly remodelled as a residential clinic and we've refurbished the old stables as a training centre and kennels.'

'No more hunts, then?'

Her brows dived together as her eyes finally met his frankly. 'You've been to Heatherglen?'

'Not for a long time.' He felt her eyes stay on him as he knelt down to give Skye another cuddle. The last thing he was going to tell her was that that long-ago day at Heatherglen was one of his handful of good memories from his childhood. Guilting her into an invitation she didn't want to give wasn't his style. Especially if it meant the ultimate outcome was helping patients with the added bonus of sticking one to Gavin Henshall. The money he'd give to see the look on Gavin's face when he found out he wouldn't get his precious car park.

'So…' Esme's voice trickled down his spine again. 'Does this mean you're considering my offer?

He stood up and looked her square in the eye. 'If it means saving this place, let's do it. How do I get in touch with you?'

Esme shook her head. She might need her ears checked. Did Max Kirkpatrick just say he wanted to touch her?

An image pinged into her mind. Ice skating by moonlight. Her mittened hand in his bigger, stronger hand. The two of them skating away beneath the starlit sky until he pulled her to him and… She screwed her eyes shut and forced the image back where it had come from.

'Email? Phone?' he prompted.

Oh. Right. That kind of contact. She handed him a card. 'From here it's pretty easy. We'll do two video calls with you and the patients once you've picked them.'

'For what purpose?'

'It's how we introduce the dogs to the patients before training at Heatherglen gets under way. It gives me a good feel for who they are before they arrive. If you could take part in the calls, that would be greatly appreciated.'

'Why do you need me?'

Esme bridled. If he was going to persist in questioning every single thing she said and did, she was right to keep him away from Heatherglen. 'If a couple of video conferences and formal wear is too much of a sacrifice to secure two free, incredibly talented service dogs for patients who would normally have to wait years to receive one... I completely understand.' She gave him her most nonchalant smile, hoping it disguised just how intense she was finding all of this. The penetrating looks. The pointed questions. The downright yumminess of him. The last time someone had had this visceral effect on her... *Oof...* She shuddered as she felt Max's dark eyes continue to bore into her.

'Why do I need formal wear for a conference call?'

'It's for the Christmas ball. You're req—'
She stopped herself from saying *required*.
She didn't like being bossed around and had
the very clear impression he didn't either.
'It's really useful if the founder of the char-
ity comes along and speaks with the donors.'

'Schmooze, you mean.' A flash of a smile
appeared. 'You might want to reconsider that.
It's not really my forte.'

'So I noticed,' she said dryly.

He laughed and once again that strangely
comfortable feeling she got from banter with
him made the day seem a bit less cold.

'I can pick any patients I want?' He asked.

'Doctor's choice.' She nodded. 'The harder
the better.'

Her eyes dropped to just below his waist.

Oh, good grief.

Work. She should think of work. Work was
not sexy. Complicated patients to match to
hard-working service dogs. Also not sexy.
Big brothers. They definitely weren't sexy.
Work, complicated patients and big brothers.
Okay. Her heart rate began to decelerate. She
liked bringing in clients Charles knew nothing about. He was far too serious for his own

good and this was her annual chance to pop a little spontaneity into his life. And her own.

She followed his gaze as it drifted across to the hospital, his mind obviously spinning with options.

She got the feeling he was going to test her. Good. Maybe *this* would be the year that signing over the proceeds from the charity ball gave her back that magical feeling she'd lost all those years ago when her brother had been killed in action, she'd married a hustler and just about everything else in her life had imploded.

'You're not going to bend on the Christmas ball thing, are you?' A smile teased at the corners of his mouth.

'Nope!' She grinned. 'And let me know if you don't have a tuxedo. You'll need one for the ball.' She gave him what she hoped was a neutral top-to-toe scan. 'You'd probably fit into one of my brother's if you don't have one. I'm sure we could stuff socks in the shoulders if you don't fill it out.'

What was she on? He'd make a fig leaf look good. Which was an image she really shouldn't let float around her head quite as gaily as it was.

'If I go formal, I wear a kilt, thank you very much.'

A kilt! Yum. She had a weakness for a Scotsman in formal kilted attire. Her brain instantly started undressing and redressing him. What she saw she liked very much. Too much. Was it too late to uninvite him to the ball as well?

Yes. Yes, it was. Besides, as much as seeing Max Kirkpatrick in a kilt could very well tip her into the danger zone of dating outside her brother's 'pre-approved' choices... she needed him. The donors loved hearing about the charities from the founder.

'A kilt will do very nicely,' she said primly.

He gave her a sharp sidelong glance as if he'd been following her complicated train of thought, then took a step back and said, rather formally for someone who'd just been flinging about witty banter, 'In which case, Ms Ross-Wylde, I'd be delighted to accept your offer to participate in two phone calls and the ball.'

It was a pointed comment. One that made

it clear he'd understood loud and clear she hadn't asked him up to Heatherglen. A wash of disappointment swept through Esme so hard and fast she barely managed to keep her smile pinned in place as she rejigged her vision of what the next few weeks held in store. Training patients. Absolutely normal. The hectic build-up to Christmas. Ditto. The Christmas carnival being set up out at the front of the castle that would, once again, be a good opportunity to practise with the dogs and their handlers.

It was ridiculous of her to have imagined for as much as a second that she might finally make good on that fantasy to skate by moonlight, hand in hand, with someone who genuinely liked her for herself. Let alone share a starlit kiss.

'Delightful.' Brisk efficiency was the only way she'd get out of this garden with a modicum of her dignity intact. She called Skye to her side. 'We'll expect them on the fifteenth and you on the twenty-third in Glasgow.'

She turned and gave a wave over her shoulder so he wouldn't see the smile drop from her lips.

Stupid, stupid girl. The last time she'd let her heart rule her actions she'd ended up humiliated and alone. She'd been a fool for letting herself think that Max Kirkpatrick could be the one who would bring that sparkle of joy back into Christmas.

CHAPTER TWO

MAX WASN'T SURE who was more nervous. Him or the twelve-year-old kid squirming like a wriggly octopus on the wheelchair beside him. His eyes flicked to the chair behind them. Euan's mum was there. Carly. Timid as ever. Gnawing on a non-existent fingernail, her eyes darting around the office he'd managed to commandeer for the video call.

The poor woman. She didn't look as though she'd had a good night's sleep in years. The same as his mum back in the pre-dictator days. Getting Carly here today had been a feat and a half. How on earth she was going to get two weeks off work was beyond him.

'You ready for this?' Max asked. He wasn't. He was no stranger to sleepless nights, but he definitely wasn't used to erotic dreams. Or a guilty conscience. There was a hell of a lot more information he should've told Esme that would've explained his spiky behaviour when she'd appeared at Plants to Paws last week, but having jammed himself into an emotion-proof vest quite a few years back, sharing didn't come easily. Sharing meant being closer to someone. Opening up his heart. There was no point in doing that because he'd learnt more than most that opening up your heart and trusting a person meant someone else got to kick the door shut.

It had happened with Gavin. And with his fiancée. Now very much an ex-fiancée. And out on the battlefields of Afghanistan where lives had been lost because he'd trusted his commanding officer and not his gut.

He gave Euan and Carly as reassuring a smile as he could. They were living breathing reminders that if everything Max had been through hadn't come to pass, Plants to Paws wouldn't exist and Euan wouldn't be getting this once-in-a-lifetime chance to get his life back on track. Not the world's best silver lining, but… *'Start small, aim high.'* One of his mum's better sayings. *'Forgive him, Max…'* being one of the worst. There was no chance Gavin Henshall deserved his forgiveness. Not after everything he'd done.

Euan's mum fretted at the hem of her super-market uniform. 'Could you run us through what the call's going to involve again, please?'

'Absolutely. It'll be similar to the one Fenel-la's going to have tomorrow.'

'She's the poor woman with epilepsy?'

Max nodded. Fenella had first came into A and E on a stretcher after a horrific car accident. Since then the forty-one-year-old had come in with cuts and bumps after experiencing severe epileptic seizures resulting from the head trauma she'd suffered. The poor woman was nearly housebound with fear. A service dog could change her life.

'She'll be getting a dog specifically trained for her requirements.'

'And Euan's dog will be trained to help with his...situation?' Carly asked.

Bless her. She never could bring herself to say PTSD.

'My crazy brain, Mum. My *crazy* brain!' Euan pulled a wild face and waggled his hands.

The poor woman looked away. She blamed herself for what her son was going through, as parents so often did, when, in reality, the attack on Euan had simply been very, very bad luck. The kind of bad luck that could change his life for ever.

Max looked Euan square in the eye. 'Esme knows what happened and will find a dog that can be there for you. It'll make being at home on your own more relaxing.' He glanced at Esme's email again, trying not to picture her lips pushing out into a perfect moue as she concentrated. He cleared his throat and continued. 'She mentions having a chat with the headmaster at your school. Some therapy dogs are permitted, so…if you need it, he might be coming along to school with you.'

Euan's antsy behaviour suddenly stilled. The poor kid. The past couple of times he'd shown up in A and E had been for black eyes and cuts from fights at school. Despite the best efforts of the headmaster, it definitely wasn't Euan's safe place.

His story set the bar for cruel cases of mistaken identity. He'd been walking home from school about eighteen months ago when a local gang had mistaken him for someone else and had near enough pulverised the life out of the poor blighter.

Even in the war zones he'd been in, Max struggled to remember a kid who'd met the wrong end of a fist to such ill effect. He was a poster boy for PTSD. He bunked off school regularly. He had frequent panic attacks. His nightmares woke everyone in the flats around them, the screams were so piercing.

Carly was a single mum and worked shift hours so couldn't be there for him when he needed it most. He was a scared kid with no one to back him up and the only way he knew how to deal with all that fear was rage. With waiting lists longer than Max's arm, Euan needed someone beyond the psychiatric profession on his side. Someone to give him a bit of confidence. A reason to see the bright side of life. Someone with the unerring loyalty of a dog.

Max glanced up at the clock. 'Right. It'll be a short call. Enough time to meet the dog, find out his or her name.'

'I hope it's a boy. A huge bulldog!' Euan's eyes gleamed with possibility.

'There's only one way to find out.' Max pressed the button and waited for Esme to answer.

* * *

Seeing Max Kirkpatrick's face appear on her screen brought back a whole raft of emotions Esme thought she had dismissed a week ago. So she'd thought he was hot. So what? Lots of people were hot. Like…um…movie stars. And models. And ex-soldiers with dangerously sexy hair working in inner-city A and Es who were doing their damnedest to keep their hearts off their sleeves.

But now that she was seeing him again?

Heart hammering. An entire swarm of butterflies careering round her tummy. A flock of birds might as well have been circling her head. She tore her eyes away and did her best to focus on the young lad sitting next to Mr Extra-Gorgeous with a cherry on top.

The boy he'd selected, Euan Thurrock, really pulled at her heartstrings. Skinny. Buzz cut. Looked ready for a fight, but it was so easy to tell there was a scared little boy hiding beneath all of that bravura. She couldn't imagine having to live in the same neighbourhood where he'd nearly lost his life. When the proverbial rubbish had hit the fan when she'd lived in Glasgow, she'd had a five-thousand-acre estate to hide in. Euan had to confront his biggest fears on a daily basis. She wasn't entirely sure she ever had.

She glanced at Max then looked back at Euan. 'So, are you ready to meet Ajax?'

Euan punched the air. 'Ajax sounds awesome. Like an attack dog. Is he a Rottweiler? A Doberman Pincer?'

Esme smiled. 'None of the above, I'm afraid.' She whistled the dog over and watched Euan's face melt with affection when the golden Lab popped his furry face up to the screen. 'Euan, meet Ajax.'

Despite having done 'the big reveal' hundreds of times, Esme felt the familiar sheen of tears glaze her eyes. It wasn't just the dog's adorable face as it tried to make sense of what it was seeing on the screen, and this dog was particularly adorable. Dark brown eyes, black nose, fluffy golden fur and ears that quirked inquisitively at any unfamiliar sounds. It was Euan's face that caught her heart and squeezed a few extra beats out of it.

Seeing this tough kid's eyes light up to see something that represented hope would've turned anyone into a puddle. It was an expression that said he believed someone was finally, unequivocally on his side.

She gave Ajax a treat then asked him to sit beside her. 'So, Euan, d'you mind introducing me to your mum? She's the adult coming to stay with you, right?'

Euan's mum gave a nervous wave as Max and Euan pulled their chairs apart to make room for her to scoot forward. 'This is Carly,' Max said, his voice a bit thick with emotion if she wasn't mistaken. 'She's all booked up to join Euan next week.'

'Actually...' Carly put her hand to her mouth then dropped it '... I've got a wee problem on that front.'

Max's eyes went wide with concern. 'Is everything all right?'

She shook her head. 'My bosses have pretty much said if I leave at this time of year, I can expect not to have a job when I get back.'

Esme was shocked. She always covered costs and rarely had problems with employers. 'Would you like me to make a call?'

Carly shook her head again. She looked as timorous as she was sure Euan felt. 'I don't want to make a fuss. I'm afraid the job's a bit more important than the dog.'

Esme bit down on the inside of her cheek. If only she'd had the training centre in Glasgow, as she'd planned all those years ago.

If only the world was populated by nice, honest men who didn't spend their new bride's trust fund on nightclubs instead of training centres.

Before she had a chance to say anything, Max jumped in. 'I'll go.'

The look of sheer gratitude Euan threw him near enough tore Esme's heart out of her chest. When Euan got himself together enough to give Max a fist bump, neither of them managed to meet the other's eye.

Esme's chin began to wobble. She cupped her hands over her mouth.

Max straightened up, looked back at the video screen and what felt like straight into Esme's soul. 'If that's all right? Wouldn't want to mess around your well-laid plans.'

There was an edge to his voice, but it was a protective one. An edge that spoke of a fierce protectiveness that wasn't going to let Euan experience one more disappointment.

If Esme hadn't fancied Max before, she... well, she was really going to have to command her heartstrings into place. No fawning, or drooling, or looking with dopey-eyed fondness at a man who so clearly wanted to be warm, kind and open but, for whatever reason, couldn't.

One week ago, her instinct had been to keep him as far away as possible.

In the last five seconds her entire nervous system had done a one eighty. Take away the rugged good looks, the hands she would've paid money to see hold a puppy and that chestnut hair just begging her fingers to play with it—and underneath it all was a solid, reliable and trustworthy man.

Which was perfect. So long as he stayed at the end of a video call. Which was no longer happening.

Right! So. She started a mental to-do list with just one very important item: do not fall head over heels in love with Max Kirkpatrick.

This was her most vulnerable time of year and, as such, she had to be on her guard.

'So!' She scribbled some nonsense onto a pad no one could see then gave Max a bright smile. 'Just a few little rules and regs to cover.'

'I would expect nothing less,' he said with a…oh, my…rather sexy smile. The type that said he could see right through her and back again.

Rule number one was going to be tough.

Esme gave what she hoped was a briskly efficient nod and ran through a few things, including what clothes to bring, what sort of weather to expect and asking about any dietary requirements.

Max looked at Euan. 'I think just about anything beyond a sausage roll will be a new one on this lad.'

Euan jabbed him in the ribs. 'I'm not that bad. I've heard of…um…sushi.' He abruptly leant in and whispered something to Max.

Max answered quietly then gave the lad's head a slightly awkward scrub. 'Maybe we can scratch the sushi.' The two of them threw each other a shy grin.

If there was any time to wish for some Christmas magic, now was it. Esme had a feeling it wasn't just Euan who needed a bit of TLC from a service dog. Max looked as though he had a wound or two himself that could do with being salved.

Esme glanced down at the stray pup one of their physios had found who was curled up at her feet. Dougal. Maybe she could convince Max to give him a forever home? Dougal was cuddly and responsive enough that he'd easily be a therapy dog, but…

When she looked back up at the screen Max was all business. Times. Schedules. Anything else they needed to bring. She answered his questions as efficiently as possible, all the while telling her hammering heart that she could do this. She could survive a week with Max Kirkpatrick. Besides, the second her brother Charles laid eyes on him she knew he wouldn't pass the big brother approval check list. Not that Charles was officially in charge of who she dated but having a second opinion after her disastrous elopement had seemed pretty wise, all things considered.

She followed Max's hand as it stuffed a few of his wayward curls back into submission.

What Charles didn't know…

As they signed off, Esme looked out the window towards the castle, merrily twinkling away in the early evening gloaming. It looked like something out of a fairy-tale. It was far too easy to imagine that long dreamed-of kiss under the starlight with all of the glittery warmth still swirling round her chest. Glittery warmth brought to life by one dark-haired, reluctant hero.

Good grief.

What had she just agreed to?

'How long's it going to take, Doc?'

Max gave his back-seat passenger a quick glance. 'As long as it takes, Euan.'

About eight days with any luck. Then he wouldn't have to go through the hoop-jumping Esme had no doubt set up for him. Attending Euan's training classes. Ensuring Fenella, his other 'volunteer', was all right as her elderly mother couldn't come along either, owing to previous commitments. Day in. Day out. Dining together. Training together. 'Fun time.' Whatever the hell that was. Together.

Bonding.

He didn't bond. He assessed, treated, then moved on. Precisely why he'd opted to work in A and E after hanging up his camos. Move 'em in, move 'em out. Zero time to bond.

Bonding made you start Plants to Paws, mate. You're going to have to own it one day.

Unbidden, an image of Esme introducing the dogs via the video call to Euan and Fenella popped into his head. He was pretty sure he was the only one who'd caught the little surreptitious swipes she'd made at her cheeks when the patients' eyes had first lit on the pooches. He was positive he was the only one in the room who'd itched to reach out and wipe them away.

'D'you think Ajax is going to be allowed in the castle?'

'How would I know? Do I look like I was raised in a castle?'

Euan snorted then asked, 'Hey, Doc, I was supposed to do a maths quiz today. Epic thanks for getting me out of school, mate!'

Max glanced into the rear-view mirror of his clunky old four-by-four and meet the lad's eyes. 'I'm not your mate and this isn't a jolly, pal. There will be homework tonight. Of that you can be sure.'

'Why're you so tetchy?' Euan countered

in a tone that suggested he was well used to cranky adults.

'I'm not tetchy.' Max's knuckles whitened against the steering wheel.

'Actually,' Fenella gently cut in, 'you are a bit tetchy.'

Max harrumphed. Whatever. So he was a bit out of sorts. Spending a week with a fairy dogmother who, via numerous phone and video calls, had managed to do all sorts of things to the steel walls he'd built round his psyche wasn't exactly something he'd been looking forward to.

Not to mention the annoyingly inviting visions that kept popping into his head of Esme in a ski suit. Esme in a onesie sprawled in front of a roaring fire. Esme in nothing at all.

He pulled off the multi-lane motorway that led north from Glasgow. The fastest option. 'We'll go the scenic route,' he growled.

Esme checked her watch. Again.

'The more you look, the longer he'll be,' her colleague Margaret teased, then gave Esme's shoulder a little pat. 'Don't worry. Lover boy will be here soon.'

Esme gave a dismissive click of her tongue. Good thing they were friends as well as co-workers.

'He's *not* lover boy! And I'm definitely *not* worried.' Esme flounced away from the window. Worry wasn't her problem. Lust was. And the last person she was going to tell was Margaret—a woman on a single-track mission to get Esme to date someone 'interesting'. Just because Margaret was now madly in love, it didn't mean Esme had to be as well.

'What's he like? Your sexy doc? And don't trot out the line about how you can't say until Charles meets him because we both know what the men he approves of are like.' She feigned an enormous yawn to show just how interesting she thought his choices were.

Esme laughed. Her brother did have a tendency towards introducing her to men who… well…lacked lustre, but she'd told him she wanted a man who didn't have a single surprising thing about him. He'd taken her at her word. Not that he played cupid all that often, but when he did? Suffice it to say there had yet to be a love match.

'Ez? C'mon. Details, please.'

'I told you. He's a Glaswegian A and E doctor.' With gorgeously curly brown hair and the darkest, most fathomless brown eyes she'd ever seen. He'd been a bit stubbly when they'd had their last video call. She could just imagine his cheek rasping against hers when he— No! No, she could not.

Margaret grabbed a gingerbread man from the tray Mrs Renwick, Heatherglen's long-term cook, had given the therapy centre staff and held it in front of her face. 'Won't you tell your dear friend Mags something more interesting about the big handsome doctor?'

'Who said anything about him being handsome?'

Margaret just about killed herself laughing. 'You didn't have to. The way your cheeks go bright pink each time you come off a video call with him tells me everything I need to know.' She began to chant in a sing-song voice, 'Esme needs some mistletoe!'

Esme picked up another gingerbread man and stuffed it into her friend's open mouth.

'Do not.'

Margaret tugged on her staff hoodie. When her head reappeared she grinned. 'Suit yourself.' She pulled on a gilet over her hoodie. 'I'll see for myself in a few seconds.' She flicked her thumb towards the window. 'Lover boy's here!' Before Esme could protest—again— Margaret was on her way out the door, saying she'd get the dogs ready.

Esme tried to ignore the tiny tremor in her hand as she took a distracted bite of the gingerbread man, her eyes glued to the battered four by four that would give their new vet Aksel's bashed-up staff vehicle a run for its money. His arrival had been a godsend at the busy veterinary clinic. Running it and the canine therapy centre was a Herculean task and Aksel tackled everything Esme put his way with a fabulous mix of pragmatism and care. Mind you. Aksel was so loved up these days they could've issued him a wheelbarrow and a workload for ten men and he would've accepted with a smile.

Her thoughts landed in a no-go zone. It was a bit too easy to picture Max gazing at her in the same adoring way Aksel lit up whenever Flora, the rehab centre's physio, appeared.

The last time Esme had looked at some-one like that she'd lost her heart and hundreds of thousands of pounds of her family's money. Not to mention her dignity, sense of self-worth and, yes, she might as well admit it, since the divorce papers had been finalised, nearly nine years ago now, she'd found it hard to believe she was worthy of love. All the compliments Harding, her ex-husband, had lavished on her had turned out to be lies. Lies she'd vowed never to fall for again.

Her tummy flipped when she caught a glimpse of Max behind the wheel.

She bit the head off the gingerbread man.

The next week was going to be a test of sheer willpower.

Via the Clyde's administrator, she'd learnt that Max had done several tours in the Middle East. Two more than her big brother, Nick had done. As a surgeon in conflict zones he would've seen enough horror to make that difficult-to-read face of his even more practised—giving away no more than he was comfortable with, which, in her case, was just about nothing.

She'd get there in the end. She always did. She loved teasing apart the complicated webs of her clients' personalities. Not that she ever bothered turning the mirror on herself. She knew what her problems were. Trust. Trust. And trust.

The car slowed as it climbed up the hill towards the castle. She craned her neck to watch as the passengers rolled down their windows and took a look. Max was the only one not to stick his head out of the window. As ridiculous as it was, she was a bit put out. Heatherglen Castle was more than a pile of rocks thrown together to impressive effect. It was her home.

The huge stone structure was framed by a crisp blue sky, the dozen or so chimneys puffing away with fires as the weather had turned so cold. Though some of the rooms were enormous, she and her brother had done their absolute best to make the castle feel as cosy and inviting as possible for the residents. Residents like Max who—because they were running at capacity—would be sleeping in her and Charles's private wing. Just. Down. The. Corridor. When they'd put Euan's mum there it hadn't been a problem. When the thirty-something mum had turned into Mr Tall Dark and Utterly Off Limits, Esme's stomach had swirled with far too much delight.

Silly stomach. Just because a good-looking man is on the grounds, it's no reason to behave like a goofy lust-struck teen.

The car pulled up outside the clinic.

Right! Time to get to work.

Hamish, Mrs Renwick's grandson, tucked a stack of files under his arm as she walked into the reception area then pointed at her jumper. 'You going to leave any of those for us?'

She flashed him a guilty smile when she saw the crumbs. 'Of course, silly billy. I was just doing a quality control test.'

'Of Nan's biscuits?' He didn't bother to disguise his disbelief that she could say such an outrageous thing.

Her guilty smile turned sheepish. They all knew Mrs Renwick's biscuits were insanely delicious.

'Can you take this plate back to the pooches, please, Hamish?' She handed him a platter of dog-bone-shaped biscuits made to a special dog-friendly recipe. 'Make sure Dougal gets one. He adores them!'

'Aye aye, boss.' Hamish gave her a jaunty salute and headed back to the kennels. He was openly enjoying his work experience at the clinic. She hoped he followed up his dream of becoming a vet one day.

She hurriedly wiped the gingerbread crumbs off her jumper and tuned into the loud laugh of a boy as the door opened and banged shut. Euan. A woman's delighted giggle followed up the boy's. *That would be Fenella.* Good to hear everyone was in such a good mood.

Before she could come out from behind the reception desk the door to the clinic flew open, slammed against the doorstop and whacked back again, only to meet a human doorstop. She shivered against the blast of cold air and looked across in time to catch the divot between Max Kirkpatrick's eyebrows furrow in apology. 'The door caught a draught.' He scanned the large reception area in slow motion. There were the usual accoutrements of a veterinary clinic. Dog food displays. A wall full of indestructible toys. Educational posters.

As Max's eyes narrowed and the divot between his eyebrows deepened, she suddenly saw what he saw. An insane riot of Christmas decorations covering absolutely everything. Hamish may have gone a bit OTT with the tinsel and glittery snowflakes. 'You certainly like your Christmas decor,' he said dryly.

'Not your cup of tea?'

'Not so much.'

She gave a nonchalant shrug. Drowning in tinsel wasn't everyone's idea of Yuletide joy. She was more of a warm twinkly lights and a few well-placed baubles girl herself but ever since Nick had been killed on Christmas Eve and the news of his death had reached them on Christmas Day thirteen long years ago, she'd struggled to recapture the love she'd always had for the festive season.

She glanced behind him. 'Where're your patients?'

'Outside.' He flicked his thumb over his shoulders, those dark eyes of his not leaving hers for as much as a millisecond. 'They're having a snowball fight.'

'Brilliant!' She clapped her hands. 'Some say it's good for the soul.'

'Some say it's good for getting pneumonia.'

His eyes left hers and landed on her jumper. It featured three polar bears ice skating along a river up to the North Pole. 'Nice jumper.' His eyes were not on her belly button.

'Thanks.' She tilted her head, forcing his eyes back up to meet hers. 'I bought it in town if you want one.'

'It isn't my usual colour palette.'

She snorted. The man was dressed in top to toe navy blue.

'At least you're honest.'

'Some say to a fault.' He dropped her a wink that, judging from his follow-up expression, he hadn't planned to drop.

Esme looked straight into his eyes and just as they had that first time they'd met, they released a hot, sweet glittery heat that swept through her bloodstream with a not-too-subtle message. Max Kirkpatrick floated her boat. She gave herself a little shake. This wasn't a dating session, it was the beginning of a series of rigorous training sessions for the dogs and the new residents. And yet...

She forced her cheeky grin into a look of pure innocence. 'Any chance you're open to being converted? To the Christmas thing?'

A shadow tamped out the glints of fun in his dark eyes. 'I'd say about as likely as one of Santa's reindeer swooping down and taking me for a ride.'

No wiggle room in that response.

She rolled her shoulders beneath the thick wool of her jumper. Rough against smooth. Would she feel the same sensation if Max were to slip his hands…? *Stop that!*

She wove her fingers together and adopted a pious expression as she began the lie she told herself every year. 'I happen to love Christmas and all of the ancillary—' her voice dropped an octave '—*accoutrements.*'

They both looked surprised at her foray into 'bedroom voice'. No one more so than Esme. The last thing Christmas was was sexy. Hot chocolate, cosy fires and Christmas trees, definitely. Sultry voices and shoulder wriggles in silly Christmas jumpers? Not even close.

The fact she even looked forward to the holiday was little short of a miracle.

Ever since Nick's commanding officer had shown up at their front door on Christmas Day all those years ago, Esme had been trying to convince herself it was still the best day of the year. Impossible when they'd been told the rebel forces had taken advantage of the holiday to set intricately built tripwire bombs across the village where Nick had been stationed. Even tougher when they'd found out the only reason Nick had been out and about had been to deliver presents to a bunch of young soldiers who'd been finding it tough to be so far away from home.

Ever since that day Christmas had been like participating in a dreary panto. Each of them going through the motions, pretending they were happy, when all they wanted to do was weep for the golden boy they'd lost. Not that 'they' were much of a they any more. Esme's doomed romance had taken up the first year after Nick's death.

Her mother had reshaped her grief into a near pathological need to enjoy life. Parties, swanning around the globe, scandalous affairs that had quickly led to the end of her parents' long and happy marriage. Her father had passed away three years after Nick had and their mother was now married to a Greek shipping magnate, so it was just Esme and

Charles now, neither one of them doing all that well at re-injecting joy into Christmas.

No doubt as a former soldier, Max had his own particular days he didn't like. Unlike her, he didn't seem all that interested in trying to tap into any tendrils of Christmas cheer lurking somewhere in his heart. For the past thirteen years it had been like a mission for her. Which maybe defeated the purpose—pounding a square peg into a round hole—but there was something about Christmas that sang to her and she wanted to find that music again.

From a very early age she had believed that Christmas was magical. The decorations, the frenzied build-up, the secrets. More than any of those, though, she'd always loved the *giving*. Much more than the receiving. Seeing the joy on someone's face when they opened an unexpected present, or a child who had their first proper spin round the ice rink at the Christmas carnival, or someone's eyes widening as the first snowflake of the season landed on their mittened palm...she loved it. She just wished that the joy of the season touched her heart the way it used to.

All of which reminded her... She lifted up

the tray of biscuits resting on the counter. 'Are you so anti-Christmas that you'd refuse a homemade gingerbread man?'

Max rolled his eyes at her as if she were the lost cause.

Well, to each his own. At least he knew his mind. Honesty was clearly his policy and he stuck to it even if it did make him look like a Scrooge. She could respect that. A slow grin crept back onto her lips. Even Scrooge saw the light in the end.

CHAPTER THREE

TWO SECONDS.

Two measly seconds was all it took for Max to start working on an exit plan. Impossible, given his idiotic instinct to volunteer as Euan's guardian, but how the hell was he meant to survive? Esme was a walking, talking Christmas minx. One who, without as much as a how do you do, had him dropping winks and staring at her boobs. Classy. He really suited the whole 'landed gentry' surroundings. Not.

If he didn't watch himself he'd have her over his shoulder, out the door and high-tailing it around Heatherglen on a quest for mistletoe. He'd bet her lips tasted like peppermint. Or whatever it was Christmas was meant to taste of.

Sugar and spice and all sorts of things that were wickedly nice.

He stuffed his hands in his pockets. He

shouldn't be thinking about what anybody's lips tasted of. He should be thinking about Euan and Fenella and their dogs and the time he'd no longer have to spend with them in A and E because of this excellent opportunity to turn their lives around. A much more practical line of thought.

A woman wearing a gilet with her name and the therapy centre's logo stitched onto it pushed through the swinging doors that led to the kennels. Margaret. She was thirty-something. Dark-haired. Rosy-cheeked, from the cold most likely. Her eyes pinged from Esme to Max then back again. Margaret smirked. Esme glared.

If he was any good at reading women's signals and, like his flirting skills, they were rusty, Max would've bet cold hard cash Esme had told her that he was a crusty old man. Esme had obviously lied. Not that he slathered himself in youth potion or hunky man juice or anything, but he was relatively confident he was a step up from the abominable snowman's granddad.

Perhaps the exchange of meaningful looks

between the women meant Esme was staking a claim on him.

He quickly pulled the plug on that idea. Esme was a beautiful woman and an heiress. She doubtless had queues of men ready to slip a ring on her finger.

Something instinctive told him the socialite scene wasn't her gig. Anyone who announced she picked up poo wasn't someone who fancied being a pretty bauble for some man to parade around on his arm. Maybe that was why her clinic was hidden away up here in the Highlands. Down in Glasgow or Edinburgh she could be at the doorstep of so many more people who would benefit from her therapy dogs. He had something teasing at his memory he couldn't quite bring to mind. Something he'd skidded over on the internet when he had been researching her work here at Heatherglen. A romance gone bad, perhaps? Whatever. Not his business.

As if she'd been reading his mind and wanted the thoughts to stop, Esme cleared her throat.

'Margaret,' Esme said pointedly, 'may I

introduce you to the man behind Plants to Paws, Max Kirkpatrick?'

'Hello, Max,' Margaret said, a merry twinkle in her bright blue eyes. 'It's *very* nice to meet you. Esme simply hasn't been able to stop talking—'

Before Margaret could elaborate, Esme cut in with a very polite, stagey voice, making great use of her enunciation skills. 'Margaret, don't you think it would be lovely if we got the dogs ready to meet the new residents? Max here was just on his way to get them.'

Margaret's eyes pinged between the pair of them before she answered in the same stagey, highly enunciated voice, 'Why, yes, Esme, I think it *would* be lovely.'

'Great!' Esme gave a decisive nod. Margaret didn't move. Esme tilted her head towards the kennels.

Margaret threw an apologetic look in Max's direction. 'We normally wait for the residents to be in the room before we bring the dogs in.'

He took that as his cue to leave. Which was just as well, because it was all he could do to keep a straight face. Not that he was certain the women were having a non-verbal *he's mine* fight over him, but…it certainly felt that way. It'd been a hell of a long time since anyone had played tug of war for his attentions. No offence to Margaret, but if he were remotely interested in having his heart shredded to smithereens again, he knew which way the pendulum would swing. Not that falling for Esme was an option.

He'd adored his ex. Had loved her to within an inch of his life. She'd been all for his plan to save up money to buy his mum a house. Had supported his extra tours of duty. The overtime. The delayed returns. He'd thought she was amazing. Right up until he'd discovered her largesse was easier to bear because she'd been having a full-on affair with her boss. Not that she'd offered him the ring back or anything, but the fewer reminders of what it was like to have his emotions in someone else's power the better.

After he'd managed to brush most of the snow out of Fenella's hair and Euan's hood, they went back to the reception area, where

Esme was wearing a very professional, very controlled smile.

They made a quick exchange of names, handshakes and the obligatory offering of gingerbread men. Both Euan and Fenella were so excited they could barely stand still.

'Have you had a chance to settle into your rooms yet?'

Fenella and Euan exchanged quick looks before Fenella answered for the pair of them. 'We've not seen the barracks yet, no.'

Esme's eyes shot to Max's.

Oops. He should've warned her he might've been teasing them on the ride up. There may also have been a mention of dungeons and castle keeps.

She twisted her lips into a little moue before that cheeky grin surfaced again. She'd rumbled him. 'I think Dr Kirkpatrick may have been preparing you for a Christmas surprise.' She nodded towards the castle. 'Your rooms are in there.'

Euan threw Max an incredulous look. 'You mean we're staying in the castle?'

'Looks like it.' Max gave the back of his

neck a swift rub. It was nice to be giving good news for once.

Euan put his hand up for a fist bump. 'Result, Doc!'

Max met his fist bump and then, to make sure the kid still knew his place, pulled him into a loose headlock and gave his head a light knuckle-dusting. Euan seemed to like it. Poor guy. He didn't have a dad to rough and tumble with. Someone to have his back when he needed it. Snap. At least Max had had the military. Brothers in arms and all that.

When he looked up, he caught Esme looking at him and Euan with that soft smile of hers. One that rammed an arrow straight into his heart. It wasn't often a woman saw his soft side. Then again, it wasn't often she stuck around long enough to find out he had one. After things had gone so apocalyptically wrong with his fiancée, he had decided he wasn't built for relationships, so didn't see the point in letting a woman know he had a heart thumping in his chest. Anyway, moving on...

Esme suggested Fenella and Euan pick a

toy and a couple of bags of treats each from the display rack before they met their dogs.

Euan looked at her with disbelief. 'You mean…we just take them?' He threw an anxious look at Max.

'I told him everything was gold plated here.' Max said, as neutrally as he could. There was no chance in the universe these two could afford some of the high-end collars and doggie coats on display so he'd wanted them to know things were for looking at but not for coveting. A valuable lesson his stepdad had made a point of impressing on him right from the start. He wanted cool trainers? He'd have to earn them. No time for a job and military academy? Well, then, looked as though he'd have to do without.

Euan's eyes were practically glittering with possibilities. Max's hand went back to his wallet. He'd pay if necessary. Just the once. It was, after all, Christmas.

'They may not look like it, but these are tools that will help you work with your dog. So, while you're here, these are free,' Esme explained, without the slightest air of a have giving to the have-nots.

Max's respect for her went up another notch.

'Don't worry about stocking up on treats for ever. We'll be sending along food and treat parcels once a month to keep you going for at least the first year as we're well aware you weren't prepared for this sort of expense. If it's too much at the end of that, we'll set up a support programme. For now, though, help yourselves. Think of this as an all-inclusive Christmas pressie.'

Fenella laughed. 'Don't say that to Doc Kirkpatrick. He hates Christmas.' She put on a voice to mimic Max's. 'Nothing comes for free in this world.'

Euan guffawed and gave Max a light arm punch. 'Yeah. I tried to get him to wear some reindeer antlers on the way up and he near enough decked me.'

'Is that so?' Esme's eyebrows shot up.

'Well…not literally but, yeah.' Euan gave a very serious nod. 'Doc Kirkpatrick and Christmas are not BFFs.'

'Any particular reason?' Esme kept her tone light, but she clearly wanted to know. He couldn't blame her.

'Nope.' No one needed to know just how miserable a time of year Christmas was for him.

'He's always working double shifts at the Clyde.' Euan explained.

There was a reason for that. Double shifts didn't let the demons in. Euan was trying to give him an out. There was hope for the kid.

'All work and no play,' Fenella teased, 'makes Doc Kirkpatrick a...' She ran out of steam. 'Well, you're not exactly dull, are you?'

Max could practically see the wheels turning behind Esme's sparkling blue eyes. As if she was already gearing up to change his Scrooge-like ways. Was there a challenge the woman didn't like?

'As none of this is relevant to service dogs, shall we get cracking?'

Esme narrowed her eyes as if she was staring straight at the chip on his shoulder. Oh, hell. She wasn't actually going to try to wheedle some Christmas cheer out of him, was she? To his surprise, she gave him a nod that indicated she knew exactly what he was talking about. That she understood pain and loss and everything that came along with it but she, unlike him, was trying to muddle through to the light at the end of the tunnel.

It was the type of look that made him wonder if his approach—no light, no tunnel—was a bit too blunt. He was the first to look away.

'Right, then.' Esme clapped her hands together and pointed to the displays. 'Why don't you two get a lead each and some treats? The dogs already have specialist collars that we'd like you to use. They've tried and approved of pretty much all of the treats on the wall, so take your pick.'

Max noticed Esme sending him a curious look after another round of victory air punches from Euan. He moved in closer, lowered his voice, his eyes flicking to Euan as he spoke. 'The kid's had a rough ride. That's why I didn't tell him about staying at the castle. I like to keep expectations low. Makes anything good that happens a welcome change.'

'Ha!' Esme laughed. 'That's my policy when it comes to men!'

'Good policy,' Max said darkly. He didn't like the thought of her with other men. He also didn't like that he didn't like it. He shouldn't care and he did. Which was precisely why keeping Esme at arm's length—further if possible—was the only way he'd get through this. Basic training had been easier.

Esme shot him a look so full of hurt he knew she'd taken it the wrong way. Before he could fix it, Margaret bounced through the double doors and cheerfully interjected, 'You ready, boss?'

Esme gave herself a little shake as if it would flick the pain away. 'Absolutely. It's time for Fenella and Euan to meet their dogs in real life.'

As she turned to go there was only one thought in his mind: This was a woman he would never allow to walk away. Which was why letting her think he was a bastard was for the best.

Now that Esme had properly humiliated herself in front of Max, she was as grateful to be around the dogs as she was hoping Euan and Fenella would be. Normally this was her favourite part—introducing the dogs to their new companions. This time, though, she was still stinging from Max's glowering response to her dating comment.

What had he been trying to say? That she'd always disappoint? That she'd never be enough? Hurt became anger. How dared he? He didn't know her. Another Harding Mac-Millan. She scowled. At least he didn't seem to want anything from her.

Against her better judgement, she glanced at him. He looked away.

Oh, yes. She'd read the comment right. He had no time for her except when it suited him. At least his affection for Fenella and Euan seemed genuine.

She snorted. Honest like a dog. She loved dogs, and dogs were trainable so—

No. Don't even go there.

'Any chance we're going to get this show on the road?'

Humph! Impatient like a dog.

'If you'll follow me,' Esme snipped. Margaret went to fetch the dogs as Esme showed Euan and Fenella into a large room that was a bit like a sports hall. Big, airy, more than enough room for a large group of dogs to be trained and, of course, for their new owners to learn how to handle them.

'Now, a word of warning—mostly to Max rather than the two of you,' Esme began. 'No offence.'

He put his hands up. None taken. Of course. He was ex-military. He could take it. Then again, the look on his face when Euan had fist bumped him. It was as if he'd won the lottery. There was definitely a big old softie lurking under that tough-guy exterior of his. Probably just as well it didn't extend to her.

She forced herself into work mode.

'Right! In a wee while we'll give Max a dog too, so he can experience the same training as you are. First things first, though...your dogs are precisely that. *Your* dogs. They need to bond with you and only you.'

She scanned the small group again, her confidence growing as her professionalism came back into play.

'The most important thing to remember when you meet your dog is that you are their new best friend and you are going to establish a bond that, up until this point, they've only had with their trainer. Margaret and I are the main handlers, but we tend to raise a lot of the puppies down in the village so that they grow up in a home environment. They've been well socialised. What that means is you are going to have to make extra-sure that the praise they seek is yours. That the only treats they receive are from you. That the cuddles they want are from you. So this means, no matter how much you want to spread the love with Max…'

Her eyes flicked to his and she instantly wished they hadn't. *Spread the love?* Was she mad? No. She needed to make her own point now that he'd made his.

'You can't. No treats. No cuddles. Nothing.'

There. Line drawn.

If Esme was trying to make a point, Max heard it. Loud and clear. Any chemistry he might've felt humming between the two of them had run its course. Fair enough. He'd been a jerk. She wasn't one to beg. Good for her. Too bad he hadn't had that same ability back when he'd kept hoping his step-dad would finally realise he was a good kid, or that he had been hallucinating when his fiancée had told him there was someone else. Someone worth loving. He felt a scowl form. Being here was reopening a whole ream of memories he'd hoped to never revisit.

He made himself tune back into what Esme was saying.

'Are you ready for me to bring the dogs in?'

Euan and Fenella were so excited he thought their heads would pop off if they nodded any more vigorously. Even he had to admit it was pretty damn sweet. When Margaret brought the dogs in, it was all he could do to keep the tears at bay. And that was saying something.

Margaret dropped the lead to the biggest of the two dogs and said, 'Go, Nora. Go to Fenella!'

Fenella dropped to her knees and immediately embraced the large, creamy-haired goldendoodle. 'You're absolutely gorgeous, aren't you lovely? Look, Max! Isn't she gorgeous? No, I mean don't look. She's all mine!' Then she burst into giggles and dug into her pocket to give Nora a treat. Nora took it then licked Fenella's face.

There it was. A forever bond made in a second.

Euan was equally over the moon. Max had thought the lad would've tried to put on more of a cavalier attitude. Pretend he kind of liked the dog. But when the big old bandy-legged golden Lab bounded over to him and offered a paw? Instant love.

Max gave his jaw a rub then shoved his hand through his hair, willing the scrubbing on his scalp to keep the bottleneck of feelings exactly where it should be. Suppressed. Churning away in his gut. Wherever. Anywhere but on display.

'It's pretty amazing, isn't it?' Esme had appeared by his side without him noticing. Little magical Christmas nymph that she was. She probably had elf dust or something like that in the small treat pouches she had hanging off her belt. 'I always cry.'

He looked down at her and, sure enough, she was wiping away a couple of tears. One glistening liquid diamond from each eye.

'How do you do it?'

Her eyebrows furrowed together. 'Match them up, you mean?'

He nodded.

'That's relatively easy. Well, you obviously

have to have the dog trained up for the right job. Then I read the profiles that you send and…' She gave an unreadable shrug. 'I just get a feeling.'

Against his better judgement, he laughed. 'Female intuition?'

Her eyes dropped to half-mast and moved from him to the dogs. 'No. Past experience, a wealth of knowledge and a finely tuned instinct for my dogs and the types of people they'd suit.'

Well, that told him.

They silently watched Fenella and Euan play with their new dogs as Margaret showed them, in turn, how to get the dogs to sit, shake paws, high five. No doubt they'd get to the 'serious stuff' in a bit. For now, it was bonding time.

Damn. He hated to admit it but these two were experiencing exactly what he had hoped would happen when his mum had told him there was a new man in both of their lives. She'd organised a picnic in Glasgow's Botanic Gardens. Proof, if he'd needed any, that this was no casual boyfriend and that he definitely wasn't from their neighbourhood.

Max had brought along a football and a chest bursting with hope that this time he and his mum might've found 'their guy', as she'd liked to put it. She'd never brought men home. Said it wasn't right as she wasn't just seeing someone for herself. It was for both of them. She'd get Max the dad he deserved after she'd made such a poor choice the first time round.

A fresh wash of guilt poured through him. He should've told Esme he knew the developer. He'd tried to convince himself it didn't matter because he would've fought whoever was trying to crush Plants to Paws. But there was a part of him that wanted to crush Gavin Henshall, too. No. Even that was wrong. Not crush, just...

'Forgive him, Max.'

He looked across at Euan, whose dog was lolling on his lap, his tongue hanging out of his mouth, his eyes glued to Euan's. He wanted that.

Bonding. He'd been desperate for it with Gavin.

And he was never going to get it.

Without his having noticed, Esme appeared

beside him, her eyes solidly on Euan and Fenella.

'I know,' she said softly. 'That's why I do this. Pure love with absolutely nothing expected in return.'

He chanced a glance in her direction and when their eyes met? He saw it. The clear-eyed gaze of someone who understood exactly what it felt like not to be enough. And at that instant he fell a little bit in love with Esme Ross-Wylde, though every part of him knew there was no chance of a happy ending. Not for guys like him. Not with girls like her.

Esme shot him that impish grin of hers. 'Right, then, pal. It's your turn.'

'My turn?'

'Yup. We've got a dog for you to do some training with, so you don't feel left out. He can stay in your room with you, just like the others' will, or he can stay here in the kennels. On his own. Crying himself to sleep at night.'

'Yeah, I don't think so.'

Esme said nothing.

'I live in a flat. I work all the time. I don't have a life that's got room for a dog.'

He decided not to remind himself that he'd made the life that didn't have room for dogs, or other humans for that matter.

'No one's asking you to fall in love with him,' Esme said neutrally. Her eyes told a different story. She was daring him not to.

'Do what you must,' Max said.

'Nice attitude, mate.'

His stepfather's voice rang loud and clear in his head. One of the many things he hadn't been able to shake from his past. The low rumbling voice. The biting quips that never failed to make him feel lower than the mud on Gavin's shoe. *Time to earn your keep, mate. Pull up your socks, mate. Off to military school, mate. Maybe they'll know what to do with you.* As if he were a lost cause before Gavin had even tried to like him, let alone love him.

Euan's laugh pulled him back into the room. He followed his eyeline, then heard Fenella get the giggles as they all watched Margaret jog in with the scruffiest puppy he'd ever seen. The little puppy was wearing miniature red velvet reindeer antlers and a jumper covered in snowflakes. He could've scooped the little mess of fur and quirky ears up in one hand and barely felt the difference. If he was into scooping up puppies and going all doe-eyed, that was.

Esme's grin split into that superstar smile of hers. 'Max? I'd like you to meet Dougal. Your very own fur buddy for the next fortnight.'

'Ha-ha, very funny. Pair the big lunk with the tiny mongrel.'

Esme feigned dismay. She picked the puppy up and nuzzled him, holding his face to hers, both of their eyes all wide and innocent. 'How on earth could you say no to this poor orphaned pup? All alone at Christmas with no one to love him?'

Hell. He knew what that felt like too. Esme was really punching each and every one of his buttons today and he wasn't even on the patient roster. He felt Euan's eyes on him and made the mistake of letting some of the hope in the lad's eyes transfer to his own heart.

'Hand him over.' He held the puppy up so they were eye to eye. 'It's you and me, pal. What do you think of that?' Dougal licked him on the nose and barked.

CHAPTER FOUR

'ALL RIGHT IF I hang out with Euan and Fenella until we set off?'

'Go for it,' Esme chirped a bit too enthusiastically, trying to resist the urge to touch Max's arm, his hand, his anything really because each time they so much as brushed a pinkie finger...fireworks. For her anyway. Twenty-four hours in and, despite her best efforts, that same heated attraction that had lit her up from the inside out the first time she'd laid eyes on him refused to be tamped down. If anything...it was worse.

She watched from a distance as Fenella and Euan showed Max the tricks they'd just learned in the clinic. They 'shot' their dogs to get them to play dead. He laughed appreciatively. Then they 'shot' him, after which he picked Euan up and tried to carry him away, only to have Euan's dog cut in and 'save' him as they'd done in one of the practice sessions.

If she hadn't known better, she would've thought he was a father trying to do his very best by his son. Did he want children of his own? Marriage? Though he came across as gruff and spiky with her, Fenella and Euan clearly adored him. They must think he was heaven sent. They probably thought a lot of things. None of which probably included being scooped up in his arms, flung onto a four-poster bed and having their wicked way with him.

Nope. She hadn't thought of that once.

He glanced over and caught her eye. The gold sparks that lit up his brown eyes whenever he let himself relax became shadowed.

Well, then. At least she knew who, of the two of them, wasn't fizzing with frissons.

'Shall we get going?' She rubbed her hands together then pointed towards the path they would be taking.

Max passed on the instructions to Euan and Fenella then walked over to her as if she were an obligation to fulfil.

Esme's heart sank a little. She didn't want to be an obligation. She wanted to be… Her breath formed into a little cloud as she huffed out a frustrated lungful of air. She wanted to be loved, that's what she wanted. What she didn't want was to have it be unreciprocated, so she needed to nip this whole *light my fire* vibe in the bud.

'The place hasn't changed much since I was here last,' Max observed.

'Oh, yes!' She clipped Dougal's lead onto his collar and tried to match Max's long-legged stride. 'I thought you'd mentioned you'd been to Heatherglen.'

He nodded soberly. 'Twenty-three years ago.'

'And how many days?' She joked.

'Seven.' There wasn't a trace of humour in his voice.

'Sounds like quite a memory.'

'It was. Is. My mum brought me here.'

About a thousand questions poured into her heart as he scanned the brightly deco-rated stalls surrounding the ice rink at the centre of the Christmas carnival. His eyes took on that faraway look she often saw in her brother when he was thinking of Nick or their father. It was almost as if she could see the memories shifting past his eyes. First the good ones…then the harsh reminder that there would never be more.

She'd been so gutted when Nick had been killed she'd entirely lost sight of who she was. Her father had become a workaholic. Charles had poured himself into med school as if his life had depended on it. Her mum had filled the empty hours with parties and, eventually, other men. She'd never felt more lonely.

She had became two people. A diligent student determined to become the very best vet she could be and a dedicated party girl who'd thought getting lost in the mayhem of yet another mad night out on the town was the only way to stem the grief she felt. Harding MacMillan, the leader of Glasgow's most elite pack of party people, had sensed her weakness, her desperation to feel loved. She'd stepped straight into his web of lies and deceit, willing it to fill the dark void of loss in her heart.

'Are the stables the only thing that you've revamped?'

Neutral territory. Phew.

'Apart from some of the medical elements we've added to the castle, you're exactly right.' Esme pulled a knitted hat out of her pocket and put it on. 'My parents were big fans of tradition so Charles and I tried to keep everything as it was. As you can see, the skating rink's a bit bigger, but...' she held her hands out as they approached the entryway to the carnival '...it's still toffee apples, chainsaw sculptures and mulled wine for all!'

Euan ran over, with Ajax in tow. 'Are we going in?'

Esme smiled at his undisguised enthusiasm. If Max had been anything like this as a kid, no wonder the memories had stuck. 'We're going to save the Christmas carnival for another time, if that's all right. We'll definitely have a go as we need to help you operate in crowds and tricky situations together. We'll also head into town one day. Maybe take you to the Christmas market. And there's always the Living Nativity to think about. Who thinks Max would make an excellent Joseph?' Esme shot him a playful smirk. Her first in the past twenty-four hours.

He shot a 'yeah, right' look back at her and there it was...that buzz of connection that crackled between them like electricity. If a right place and a right time for a kiss presented itself…

This way danger lay.

Esme nodded at the dogs. 'Are you two all right with them? Happy with the training so far?'

A chorus of 'Yes' and enthusiastic 'More than' filled the wintry air. Esme and Margaret had already done a lot of one-to-one work with them. Esme focused on the drills Fenella's seizure dog knew whilst Margaret had been tasked with showing Euan all the tricks of the trade his dog could help him with when he was feeling panicky or depressed.

The grin on Euan's face near enough hit ear to ear. 'I love him!' He dropped down low so he was eye to eye with the golden Labrador he had been assigned. 'Ajax and I are going to rule the world!'

Esme laughed good-naturedly. 'How about we see how the two of you do on a woodland walk first? Plenty of distractions out there. Squirrels, hares, deer. Maybe reindeer.'

Ajax gave Euan's face a lick and when he raised a paw to shake hands with the boy, he laughed without an ounce of the self-consciousness he'd arrived with. Now, *that* was satisfying.

'Do I have to keep my dog on a lead?' Fenella asked.

Esme nodded. 'Everything we're going to be doing for the next week ensures you are developing a relationship with your dog.'

'Do you think Ajax would like cake?' Euan's gaze travelled over to a parade of food stalls at the Christmas carnival. 'I love cake.'

Esme laughed. 'Cake is definitely not on their menu. Think of Ajax as an athlete. You want him to be in top health, right?' Euan nodded solemnly and blocked Ajax's view of the cake stall. It was easy to see he would let no harm come to his new furry friend.

Esme pointed to a path leading off into the woods. 'I thought we could go down to the pond for now. Another big lure for Labs and goldendoodles. Even in the winter. But re-member! You're in charge. Let's see how well you two can do at making sure they resist all of the temptations along the way.'

She held out a lead to Max. At the end of

the lead was Dougal wearing yet another Christmas jumper. 'Happy to tag along with me and Wylie as back-up?'

Wylie was a huge old St Bernard who leant in protectively towards Esme's leg. When Max didn't immediately take the lead, a thought struck her. 'Are you all right with dogs? I can't believe I didn't ask. With Plants to Paws I just assumed.'

'No, it's not that.'

'What is it?'

Max tilted his head towards Wylie. 'Loyalty. Hard to find it these days.'

The click and cinch of eye contact that followed hit Esme hard and fast.

From the shift in his stature she knew in her very core that Max felt it, too.

When she finally spoke, she barely recognised her own voice. 'Should we get a move on? I think Fenella's got an appointment with one of the physios in an hour or so.'

Esme set off at a crisp pace, reminding herself with each step that Max wasn't here to find a new girlfriend. He was here to make sure his charity didn't get paved over. Eyes on the prize. Just like her ex had had his eyes on her family money. Suddenly, the air felt a little bit chillier.

'What sort of behaviour do they have to exhibit to be a service dog?' Max's attempt to start up some casual chitchat wasn't exactly stellar but it would definitely beat the ice-queen vibes coming from Esme.

Esme briefly considered the two dogs walking beside them. 'Probably the same traits it takes to be a good soldier. Commitment. Hard work. Intelligence.' She glanced at him. 'You were in the services, weren't you?'

He nodded. She'd obviously done her research. 'Army. Twelve years.'

'As a medic or a soldier?'

'Started as a soldier but worked my way into the Royal Army Medical Corps.' He hadn't been able to stand waiting for someone else to help when one of his fellow soldiers had been injured. Mashing your hand on top of a wound rarely helped. Telling them you were there for them counted for something. Listening to their final goodbyes. As a nineteen-year-old soldier with his own emotional scars, Max had wanted something practical he could do. Medicine had rescued him from the deep morass of helplessness he'd felt ever since the Dictator had entered his and his mum's lives.

'You must've seen a lot of awful things,' Esme said.

He nodded and scrubbed at the back of his neck. They all had. At least he'd been able to walk off the plane when they'd landed back in Scotland.

'Have you chatted with Andy at all?'

Max had heard Euan introducing his dog to him the first night. 'The chap in the wheelchair?'

Esme nodded.

'Euan and he seemed to have struck up a friendship and I didn't want to interfere. He has that ex-military look about him.'

'Army. He was one of my brother's best friends.'

'Charles?'

'No. Nick.' An air of sadness cloaked her words. She shot him a sad smile. 'You aren't really friends with the internet, are you?'

He shook his head. 'Not really. For twelve

years I lived and breathed the military and since then I've been deeply involved in the A and E unit. The internet fuels gossip. I don't like gossip.'

She huffed out a disbelieving laugh. 'That would make you a rare breed.'

Shards of pain lanced through those pure blue eyes of hers and if he were the sort of man who knew how to make them go away, he would've. It was a cruel reminder that the only thing he'd learnt over the years was how to push people away.

'Nick was my older brother. Much older. He was in a canine dog squad in the army and one day… Christmas Eve, actually…things didn't go so well.'

All the little pieces he'd been trying to put together fell into place. The castle as a rehab centre. The rescued mutts. The repurposed search and rescue dogs. Those intense looks she sometimes had when she held a dog close. All of this was for their brother.

'He must've been an amazing man.'

'He was my hero.'

The depth of emotion in her voice punched him right in the solar plexus, loosening up the muscles that held his own story deeply embedded in his heart. He wanted her to know she wasn't alone. That he understood pain and loss. His mum had been his best friend up until when his stepdad had entered their lives. A man whose method of putting a relatively wayward kid back on track was to ship him out to a military academy instead of letting him live in their new home, as promised. How the same man had verbally subdued his jolly, full-of-life mother into being little more than a timorous mouse, frightened to say or do anything that might embarrass her social-climber husband. As the dark thoughts accumulated, Dougal nosed his thigh. He gave the dog's head a scrub. The pooch definitely had a sensitive side. That was for sure.

As if the move had also jostled Esme, she gave herself a little shake, popped on a smile and asked, 'What made you choose the Clydebank Hospital? Pretty rough area of town.'

'It's where I grew up.'

'Oh. Um…are your parents still there?'

'Nah.' He cleared his throat because it still

choked him up to say the words. 'My mum passed. Three years ago now.'

There was no point in mentioning his father. Step or otherwise. Neither had treated his mum the way she'd deserved.

Cancer had stolen his chance to give her the house he had bought for her. It'd taken him twelve years of service to buy it outright. He'd meant it to be a refuge from the Dictator and his constant micromanagement. As far as Max knew, he'd never laid a hand on her, but guys like that knew how to bruise and hurt in other ways. Gavin had been chipping away at his mother's self-worth for years. He hadn't wanted a wife. He'd wanted someone to feel small so he could feel big. It was a miracle she'd had any confidence left at all in the end. Or the generosity in her heart to forgive a man he didn't think he ever could forgive.

At least her battle with cancer had been swift. A cruel mercy. The day she'd died, Max had put the house on the market. He'd thought of making it a shelter, but he simply hadn't had the funding to keep one up and running. He'd used the money to establish Plants to Paws instead. His mum had loved gardening. It had been the one place she'd known her husband couldn't fault her.

He needed to bring up his relationship to Gavin before a single penny came his way from Esme, but for now he was enjoying the thoughtful silence she'd chosen in lieu of asking, *And your dad?* Like her therapy dogs, she seemed to know when to push and when to back off. If he wasn't careful he'd be pouring out all his secrets but he knew more than most that putting his heart in someone else's hands was always a bad idea. So he followed Esme's earlier lead and sidestepped the real stuff.

'Where'd you find this cheeky chappie?' He pointed at Dougal.

'A couple of our staffers found him. Cass and Lyle. Someone had abandoned the poor wee thing.' She gave the dog a goofy grin and he barked his approbation. 'Up until a few days ago he was staying with our physio, Flora, but she's moving in with Aksel—the new vet—and they already have an assistance dog for his daughter, so...' Esme looked up to the wintry sky as if for inspiration.

'Because he's so young and such a little

scruffball we weren't sure he'd be up for much training, but he seems pretty adaptable. Aksel caught him trying to purr next to a cat the other day.' She laughed, her features softening as she unclipped his lead and gave him a bit of a cuddle. 'Poor Dougal. He deserves someone who will love him exactly the way he is. A little broken. A lot in need of love.'

Something told Max she was describing herself. She sure as hell was describing him. Though he could hardly believe the words as they came out of his mouth, he said them anyway. 'Want to talk about it?'

'About Dougal?' Esme knew he'd been asking about her, but she was hardly going to pour her heart out to a man who had more control over her emotions than she cared to admit. 'Nothing to say really. His past is a mystery.' Her eyes flicked towards Max. *A bit like you.* Adopting what she hoped was a fun, interested look, she asked, 'So what's your kilt like? I'm not familiar with the Kirkpatrick tartan.'

'Probably because it's Lowland. I'm guessing the Ross-Wylde tartan is—forgive the pun—cut from a different cloth.'

It was as it happened. Highlander through and through. But that didn't mean he could tar her with a brush of superiority. 'I don't use my name to get things I haven't earned.'

His eyes widened. There had definitely been bite to her bark and Max wasn't a man to stand around getting attacked. 'You certainly seem happy to use it when it comes to flinging your money about.'

Everything in her stilled.

'Don't say that.'

Max's spine realigned into ramrod position. 'Sore point?'

'Something like that.'

She saw him reeling through the possibilities of what could make the poor little rich girl so touchy about money. When she failed to explain he asked, 'Is this why you fund the charities through the ball instead of donating it all yourself? Gives you a bit of emotional clearance so you don't have to feel responsible for anyone and they don't have to come crawling to you for more?'

He was hitting close to the bone. Too close. And he wasn't bothering to sugar-coat it.

She flicked her hair out of her eyes and tucked it back underneath her hat.

'How I run the foundation is nothing for you to worry about, Max. It's a charity event, not a Princess Charming Ball.' Instead of stropping off, which she should have done, she lashed out, 'And don't think for a minute I need to find a male version of Cinderella to make me happy.'

'No?' countered Max, the space between them diminishing as the heated intensity between them increased. 'What do you need to make you happy?'

Her heart was pounding so hard she could barely hear her own thoughts let alone the sounds around them.

Someone like you?

'Max!' Euan was running towards them. 'Come fast! It's Fenella!'

Max took off with the practised speed of an athlete. Esme scooped up Dougal's lead and, as best she could, ran behind, silently adding, *Make self immune to grumpy but sexy Scottish doctors* to her list of things to do.

* * *

When Max reached the clearing, he could hardly believe what he was seeing.

Fenella's dog, Nora, was nudging herself under Fenella's head as she came to the end of a seizure.

'She was fitting, Doc.' Euan said, breathless and a bit pale from fright. 'I stuck my glove in her mouth so she wouldn't bite her tongue or anything, but she spat it out. Too mucky, I guess.'

'It's all right, pal.' Max dropped to his knees and did a quick check of Fenella's vitals. 'You've done the right thing in finding me. From the look of things, Nora here knows what she's doing.'

'Absolutely.' Euan looked awestruck. 'I know we saw her in the practice hall, but this was the real thing. It was like she knew it was going to happen.' He looked up as Esme jogged into the clearing. 'Did you know Nora makes herself into a cushion?'

Esme gave Nora a quick pet and a treat as Fenella slowly came to. 'Absolutely. That's what she's trained to do.'

Max helped Fenella sit up. 'You all right there, hun?'

The post-ictal phase was always a bit tricky. The person who'd had the seizure could feel perfectly fine or often exhibit signs similar to those of a stroke. Headaches, slurred speech, nausea and fatigue. In rare cases, some epileptics could suffer from post-ictal psychosis and suffer from paranoia or extreme fear. Usually the anomaly occurred in people who weren't taking their medication.

'Yes, I...' Fenella looked a bit confused and then, when her eyes lit on Nora, it was as if everything pinged into place. 'I felt a bit woozy and the next thing I knew, this one was being my pillow.' She ran her hand through the dog's fur and automatically reached to her pocket to get her a treat. 'Good girl. You're a clever girlie, aren't you?'

'She was!' Euan jumped in. 'Out of, like, absolutely nowhere you fainted. But you weren't fainting. You were having a seizure, I guess, and it was like Nora knew exactly what to do. She broke your fall. Then she stuck herself under your head while you were fitting. No offence, but it was really cool.'

Max glanced across at Esme. She looked concerned for Fenella but pleased her new service dog had fallen straight into her new role. She was actively avoiding eye contact with him. Served him right. He'd been an ass. Sticking his nose where it didn't belong. He should tell her about Gavin. It would break just about every rule in his play-your-cards-close-to-your-chest handbook, but he felt he owed it to her to even the emotional playing field. He got it. Sometimes things were personal. Luckily for his emotional armour, taking caring of Fenella took precedence.

'Did you take your AEDs?' Max asked. Anti-epileptic drugs helped but weren't a fail-safe, especially if they weren't taken regularly or weren't the right dosage. Having seen her in his A and E several times for sprains and cuts sustained while she'd been fitting, he knew she had struggled for years to find the right balance of medication.

'Yes.' She looked away, rubbing her elbow.

It didn't sound like a one hundred percent yes, but he wasn't going to embarrass her in front of everyone if there was a story behind her not taking it. Or, as was often the case, she might need to change meds. They weren't a one-pill-fits-all type of medicine.

'Did you hurt yourself?'

'No more than usual.' She held up a lightly scraped hand then qualified her answer. 'I probably would've cracked my head on a stone or something if it hadn't been for Nora.' She wrapped her arm round the dog and nuzzled her face into the fluffy golden-doodle's coat. After a few moments, Max quietly asked, 'What do you think set this one off?'

Fenella shot him a sheepish look. 'Lack of sleep most likely. I've been so excited the past few days, I've hardly slept a wink.'

He nodded. 'Perhaps it'd be best if we all head back to…um…'

'The castle?' filled in Esme, with the ease of someone who'd grown up in one.

Had it been more burden than blessing?

Esme glanced at her watch. 'Max mentioned you have an appointment with Flora, our physio. Shall we head back, get you a cup of tea and some quiet time before then?'

Fenella nodded, grunting a little as she sat up properly. Max reached out to steady her.

Poor woman. Had to be tough being taken by surprise by seizures just when you thought you were having the time of your life.

'Are you two still all right having your dogs with you in your rooms? We can take them back to the kennels for the afternoon if you need a break.'

They both asked if they could have their dogs stay with them. Esme grinned a naughty little sister grin.

Which did beg the question, 'Is that not *de rigueur*?' Max asked, sotto voce. 'Having the dogs in the clinic?'

'Oh, it is,' she answered breezily. 'It just annoys my brother. Speaking of him, if he has time later on, Fenella, it might be a good idea for you to meet Charles and talk through your medications.'

'It's just the one right now. I'm sure it's fine.' Fenella looked uncomfortable about the suggestion, which instantly put Max's protective streak into high gear.

'Does he know much about epilepsy?' Max asked. A bit too defensively from the look of Esme's own bristly demeanour.

'He's a neurologist, so he's pretty good

at understanding why brains work the way they do. I'm not criticising any of the medical treatment you've received at the Clydebank, Fenella. They obviously have specialists there who are helping you and Max, here, of course. I'm just covering our bases as you are our guest. We want to make sure you receive all the treatment you need. If there's anything we can do—'

'Don't worry.' Max helped Fenella get back to her feet. 'Easy does it, lassie. Why don't we take this step by step and get this woman some rest first?'

He tried to block out the sharp looks Esme kept sending him, but the odd one or two pierced straight through to his conscience. Now he definitely owed her an apology. What had got into him? Accusing her of flinging gold coins at people for her own amusement. Dismissing her sensible offer of a fresh set of eyes on Fenella's case.

If she knew even half of the reasons why he swung from one end of the emotional spectrum to the other she'd…hell, he didn't know. Send him packing most likely. It seemed to be the remit.

His stepfather had lured him in with all the bells and whistles that had appealed to a twelve-year-old kid from the wrong side of the tracks. Tickets to premier league football matches, nights out at the scary films his mother couldn't bear, slap-up meals at the finest burger joints in town. It had been kid heaven. Until it hadn't been. And had set him up for a lifetime of keeping people at arm's length until they proved they were the real deal.

Ironically, it had been Gavin's constant demands that he 'earn his keep' that had pushed him so hard in the military. Had made him the top-rate soldier and surgeon he knew he'd been. Gavin hadn't thought he had what it took? He'd vowed to show him.

He would have as well if he hadn't had a conscience. Or carried around those little-kid hopes and dreams that one day he'd be good enough. Worth loving. He supposed it had been that same little boy's belief in love that had made him blind to his fiancée's affair. Being so oblivious had made him feel every bit as weak as he'd felt when Gavin had shipped him off to military academy, instead of taking him to their new home, as he'd promised.

A few more proofs that truth and justice rarely reigned—dodgy commanding officers, innocents rigged up with IEDs, the cruelty of poverty had closed the book on the matter. Being wary of whatever met his eye was his modus operandi. Being suspicious of whatever touched his heart was critical. It hadn't exactly made him A-list boyfriend material. A handful of one-night stands he wished he hadn't had had been the clincher. So life as the Monk had begun. Which, of course, immediately made him think of all the people who were relying on him back at the Clyde to save Plants to Paws.

His conscience gave him a sharp kick in the posterior. His emotional baggage shouldn't be a factor. Normally it wasn't. Not with the chaos he encountered in A and E every day. And yet...here it was, front and centre. His hypersensitivity did beg the question, did he want Esme to think well of him?

He stuffed his hand through his hair. No need to ponder that one. It was an unequivocal *yes*. Which meant the next week was going to hoist this festive season up amongst the worst ever.

You could try being nice.

'Go on, then,' he said when Esme shot him another *look*. 'Give your brother a call.'

And there it was. The first chink in his 'don't ask for help' armour. If you don't ask, you don't need. And if you don't need, you're never disappointed. It was a little pact he'd made with himself when the Dictator had asked him to put a value on himself the very first Christmas they'd spent together. Turned out the pair of them had disagreed.

It hadn't been a very nice Christmas.

When Esme's smile of thanks hit him on full beam, he began to wonder if his pact had flaws.

CHAPTER FIVE

ESME CAREFULLY PLACED the enormous tabby back into Mrs Elsinore's arms. 'It might be an idea to cut back on Theo's treats. The extra weight could be contributing to his arthritis.'

Mrs Elsinore looked horrified. 'But, dear, we have a routine.' She talked Esme through morning treat, morning breakfast, elevenses treat, lunchtime and so on.

'No need to veer from the routine, it's more a question of reducing—' Something, or rather *someone* caught her eye just beyond the exam-room window. A six-foot someone tugging a hat over that touch-me-now hair of his. Was it time for the afternoon walk already? Not that she hadn't been counting down the seconds or anything, but the last few patients in the vet clinic had mercifully managed to steer her thoughts away from Max. Not any more!

'What was it you were saying about routine, dear?'

'Yes. Right. Routine.' Her gaze involuntarily drifted back out the window. Max was laughing at something Margaret had said. Margaret looked so relaxed and at ease with him. The total opposite of how *she'd* been. By turns uptight, weirdly flirty, downright snippy.

He glanced over towards the window and caught her eye. He raised his hand in a half-wave but turned the instant Margaret said something. Something *hilarious* from the look of things.

Ruddy Margaret.

Wait. *What?* She loved Margaret. Margaret was her friend. Her friend who had a boyfriend and was no threat at all. Not that she was feeling competitive. It wasn't as if she wanted to date him. Or press her hand to his chest to feel his heart beat. Or find out if his lips were as kissably delicious as they looked.

'Esme, dear…shall I carry on as normal, then?'

'No. I mean…cutting back a wee bit on Theo's treats would be advisable.' Esme gave her face a quick scrub with her hands. 'Apologies. I'm a bit distracted today. New residents...'

Mrs Elsinore looked out the window and smiled. 'With residents like that I think I'd be distracted, too.'

Esme blushed instantly. 'What? Him? Oh, no...he's not...'

'Don't deny it, dearie,' Mrs Elsinore tutted. 'He is. Now, if you tell me what else you want me to do with Theo that'll free you up to go on out there and be distracted a bit more up close and personal.'

Esme pretended she hadn't heard that part.

A few dietary tips and one prescription for glucosamine tablets later and Esme was pulling on her staff puffer jacket and heading out to where residents and their dogs met for the afternoon walk.

Margaret waved her over when she saw her. 'Big favour.'

'Sure.' Especially if it involved being nowhere near Max. He was currently at the far end of the barns with Hamish and Dougal. Max didn't look as pleased as Hamish was about Dougal's new Christmas jumper.

'Woohoo! Esme.' Margaret waved her hand. 'Eyes over here, please.'

'I wasn't—'

'Yes, you were. Which brings me to my favour. Do you mind taking Max for the next couple of hours?'

'What?'

'He's brilliant, but Euan keeps deferring to him for everything and we need to take a walk where Euan's sole focus is Ajax, not Captain Gorgeous.'

'He's not—'

'Esme.' Margaret stopped her cold. 'He totally is and there's absolutely nothing wrong with fancying him.'

There was. There were a thousand reasons and probably another thousand right behind those.

'Hey.' Margaret forced her friend to look at her. 'Not everyone's Harding MacMillan. Go on a walk with the man. What's the worst that could happen?'

She was about to launch into an extensive list of all of the bad things that could happen, even though Margaret knew the whole sordid story. Before she had a chance, Margaret had called Max over, explained the situation then told them where the group would be going so Max and Esme could go elsewhere.

When Margaret walked off and left the two of them standing there Max huffed out a laugh. 'Feels a bit like a set-up, doesn't it?'

'If you're not interested in taking a walk with me, I'm more than happy to take the dogs on my own.'

'Hey, easy there. I wasn't suggesting anything of the sort, I was just saying—' What was he saying? That being alone with her made his brain go all sorts of crazy? That sleeping down the corridor from her meant not sleeping at all? That he wanted her?

It was that simple.

All he had to do now was find a way to get his body to fall in line with his brain, which was telling him to step away from the beautiful woman and everything would be fine.

Esme tightened her lips then pointed towards a path. 'If we go that way towards the old castle ruins we should stay clear of them. I'm perfectly happy to go on my own, though.'

'No. I wasn't saying anything like that.'

'Well, what were you saying?'

'I was just saying your colleague has a way of making everything sound like a date whenever she matches the two of us up.'

Esme rolled her eyes then grudgingly laughed. 'Margaret has a way of doing that. She sees herself as my personal matchmaker.'

He didn't push for details, opting to let silence do the work. If she wanted to talk about her love life, she would. If she didn't, she wouldn't. As plain as that.

After about ten minutes of briskly paced walking, Esme threw up her hands. 'It isn't that I don't find you attractive, all right?'

Despite himself, Max laughed. She'd obviously been having a conversation all by herself. Again, he decided not to push for details. Lord knew, the more he was pushed, the less he wanted to say.

'I don't date clients.'

'Who said anything about dating?'

Esme glared at him. 'You did. The thing about Margaret making everything sound like a date?'

Max rubbed the back of his neck. This was

one of those complicated conversations he had no way of winning. Did he want to take her out? Not particularly. He didn't do dating. Was he attracted to her? Absolutely. More than he had been to anyone, to be honest. There was something about Esme's combination of vulnerability and fiery strength that spoke to him. A kindred spirit who may have started off in life on a different path but, like it or not, they were on the same one now.

'You're right. This is a professional relationship. Nothing more.'

'Good,' Esme said, sounding absolutely miserable. 'I'm glad we've cleared that up.'

All of a sudden, they heard someone calling out, a loud piercing scream. It sounded like a name.

Esme scooped up Dougal and took off at a run. Max did the same, with Wylie loping along in his wake. The screams stopped abruptly. Esme pointed towards a gated field. 'A lot of villagers use this field as a shortcut to get up to the ruins. Maybe someone's dog was hit. Let's tie up the dogs here. I'll ring Aksel to come and collect them and bring the four-by-four in case we need to take anyone back to the vet or the clinic.'

All the tension tightening her features over the 'dating incident' had re-formed into exacting focus. This was not a woman fazed by crisis. Once the dogs were secured and Esme had made the call, they ran across the field, Esme leading the way. When they got to the far end, Max's doctor brain kicked into high gear. A woman was curled around a grey lurcher absolutely covered in blood. She was moaning and crying her dog's name over and over. When she looked up at them, they could see she was also covered in blood. She sobbed, 'Help! Teasel's been cut!'

'Janet, it's all right. We're here now.' Esme dropped to her knees beside them. 'Are you hurt?'

'I'm not sure. I had to jump over the fence after him and I think I twisted my ankle.'

Esme shot a glance up at Max. 'If I take the dog, can you look after Janet? She works down at the pub and has had this wee thing for…what is it, Janet four and a bit years now?'

'Five!' wailed Janet. 'We were out for his birthday walkies.'

'Well, then, we'll have to make sure we look after him with extra-special care, won't we? Why don't you sit up and we can take a look?'

Max could see what Esme was doing. Putting both of the patients at ease. Her voice was calm and steady. Her energy completely soothing. Animals read humans much better than people did and Esme had an impressive ability to match her energy accordingly.

'Sure thing.' He took his fleece off. 'Here, use this for Teasel.'

Janet clung even more tightly to her dog as Esme reached out to take him. 'I'm afraid to let go. He was chasing a deer. I tried to get him to stop.'

That explained the screaming.

'When he leapt over the fence, the barbed wire snagged him.' She sobbed again. 'It's ripped a huge wound from his chest to his belly.' She tried to pull herself up to standing, still reluctant to let go of the dog. Max reached out and caught her as she stumbled. Esme deftly grabbed hold of the dog and cradled him in Max's jacket.

'All right, darlin'.' Max eased her back to

the snow-covered ground. Not ideal, but until he knew what was wrong it'd have to do. They also weren't so far away from the castle that he couldn't carry her if necessary. She was a wee snip of a thing compared to some of the muscled soldiers he'd hoisted fireman style for over a kilometre.

Esme pulled off her puffer jacket. 'Here. Use this for Janet. She's had a shock.' The dog whimpered and Janet jumped up towards him.

'Hey,' Esme soothed. 'Teasel's whimpering is a good thing. It means his windpipe is intact.'

Janet fell back to the ground using both her hands to clutch her ankle. 'I think I sprained it or something.'

Max saw blood around her ankle, swiftly rucked up her waterproofs and carried out a quick examination. She didn't have a compound fracture or any obvious cuts so that was something, but she'd need X-rays to rule out any fractures. He felt further up along Janet's leg and was satisfied that her ankle had received the brunt of the fall and nowhere else. 'You don't happen to have X-ray facilities in the clinic, do you?'

'Yes.'

'Brilliant.' He checked Janet's pulse and suggested they keep her off her leg until he could do a proper examination. 'Looks like you got your own set of cuts as well. We'll check on the status of your tetanus jabs and get these cuts cleaned up. I don't think you'll need stitches, but—'

Janet pulled her wrist out of his hand. 'I'm not leaving Teasel! What if he's nicked an artery—what if—?' Janet became consumed with tears as she considered the very worst outcome.

'Hey.' He pulled her to his side as Esme carried out her own examination. The last thing one doctor needed was another doctor's patient jumping in at what could be a delicate moment. From the look on Esme's face, it was grim.

Max cocked his ear at the sound of a vehicle.

'That'll be Aksel.' Esme didn't look up as she wrapped the dog tightly in his coat. 'He's going to be up with the dogs—can you guide him in, please? The less movement for this little guy, the better.'

'Absolutely.'

Esme could hardly believe it had barely been a couple of hours since the mere idea of going on a walk with Max had filled her with horror. Now? She would happily have him along—day or night. Not that she was always encountering incidents like this harrowing one, but if she ever had to face the eye of a storm with someone, it was Max Kirkpatrick.

His military cool and first-class medical knowledge were exactly what you would want in a crisis. He'd even showed his soft side when Janet had dissolved into tears. Dug a clean handkerchief out of his pocket and everything. The man might see himself as solid mass of impenetrable man mountain, but her gut instinct had been right. He had a heart the size of Scotland.

'How's he coming along, Esme?' Janet asked through a speaker in the viewing room.

Esme tied off the delicate stitch then looked up. 'Only a few more stitches to go and then he can have a proper rest.' It was a highly edited way of describing what had been a difficult surgery. Teasel had had to be anaesthetised while she'd assessed the extent of the tissue damage. She'd had to debride some of the most heavily damaged areas right next to the wound and multiple layers of tissue had needed suturing but, luckily, they'd avoided having to put any drains in.

Despite Esme's insistence that Teasel would be receiving the very best of care, Janet had point blank refused to leave her dog. The best she'd agreed to was sitting in the large windowed room just outside the surgical area in the veterinary clinic, with Max in attendance. It wasn't standard practice, but…as the accident had happened on Heatherglen land, Esme felt an added responsibility to both patients.

With Janet and Max looking on, Esme had poured her concentration into the surgery as she'd painstakingly stitched Teasel's shockingly long wound back together. The barbed wire had done a real number on him, from his throat to his belly. He had miraculously managed to escape nicking his jugular vein.

If he had, the nurses wouldn't be prepping a recovery kennel for him.

The nurse who was working with Esme turned off the microphone and asked, 'Shall I ask Max to try and get her to go up to Heatherglen now?'

Esme shook her head. She wasn't going to admit it, but having Max there was strangely soothing. She didn't want to have to worry about Janet while she was working on Teasel and with Max there, she didn't even feel an ounce of concern. 'It's not like it happens every day and she's been through such a shock. Teasel's her baby. I can understand her not wanting to leave him.' Dogs were family in her book. You didn't abandon family when they needed you most. Having a mother who'd abandoned ship at her lowest ebb had taught her that the hard way. Having a brother who'd been there to pick up the pieces had confirmed it.

She glanced up and caught Max's gaze. A warm heat swirled round her belly with such intensity it was as if he'd slipped his hands under her scrubs. This was not the time to be distracted. Even so, she hadn't been able to help taking the odd glimpse at him. He had either been readjusting Janet's position so that her foot was elevated, giving her a proper blood-pressure test with a pump Lyla had run down with from the clinic along with some ice packs, or running her through a ream of questions all designed to keep Janet's eyes off the rather gruesome injury.

Max was a picture of calm, quick thinking, level-headedness in what could have been a difficult situation. Mercifully Janet's injuries hadn't been serious. She had a few cuts of her own, which Max had cleaned and put antibacterial cream on before lightly dressing them. He'd also called her GP and checked on her anti-tetanus status. She'd need a booster.

Half an hour later, when Teasel was resting in his kennel and Janet had been assured for the hundredth time that he'd be asleep for the next few hours and that they'd call straight away if there was any news, she finally agreed to let Max take her in for X-rays.

Esme had only just finished up at the surgery when she saw his vehicle leaving the castle grounds heading into town—to the GP's surgery and on to Janet's, no doubt.

She looked down and realised both of her hands were pressed tightly against her pounding heart. If she didn't watch herself...

Margaret came out of the front door of the clinic and locked the door behind her. 'Fancy a drink down in the village?'

'No,' Esme said a bit more dreamily than she'd intended. 'I'm all right here.'

Margaret followed her gaze as Max's four-by-four wended its way down the long drive. 'Oh, you are in trouble!'

Yes, Esme agreed silently. Yes, she was.

Charles stopped Esme as she was about to enter the kitchen.

His big-brother expression turned serious. 'The snow's just started, it's pitch black and it's icy.'

'Thanks for the weather report, Charles.'

He gave her a don't-be-daft look. 'I'm trying to tell you it's not safe to go out driving.'

Easily falling into her role as kid sister, she shot back, 'I happen to be an excellent driver, thank you very much.'

'Where are you going all dressed up like that?'

His eyes dropped to her flirty, swishy, feminine skirt. She never wore skirts. It was usually scrubs, workout clothes or pyjama bottoms at this time of the evening, unless she was meeting Margaret in the village for a glass of wine or, on very rare occasions, heading to Fort William or Glasgow for a dinner date. Yawn-fest more like. She silently vowed never to take her brother up on another suitable suitor again.

Though her features remained stoically neutral as he waited for an answer, she could feel tiny tendrils of heat creep into her cheeks. 'I'm just on my way to see Mrs Renwick. Everything else is in the wash.'

'Yeah, right.'

'Why are you so grumpy?'

'I'm not grumpy.'

He was. He was very grumpy. Which was annoying as he'd been in an absolutely brilliant mood when he'd come back from his medical conference a couple of months ago. It'd made a nice change from Dr Too Serious for His Own Good. Maybe he should go to another one. It would keep his prying eyes away from the fact she just might have accidentally on purpose put on something slightly more feminine in case she accidentally on purpose ran into a certain Max Kirkpatrick.

Since he'd come back a couple of hours earlier it was as if they were slowly circling one another, neither one willing to make the first move. Not that she even knew what kind of move was going to be made. If they were simply going to be friends, fine. She just wanted an end to this silly friction that existed between them. Working together today had helped, but when he hadn't bothered to find her after he'd come back from town, she'd gone into another one of her insane spirals of insecurity.

Was she good enough? Wasn't she? Was it time to simply grow up and not treat every single man who showed a flicker of interest in her as a potential pariah? Maybe in this case work was work and pleasure was a figment of her imagination.

Either way, she wanted the tension to end. She respected him and there was absolutely no reason why they couldn't be friends. She gave her brother a supercilious sniff then swished through the swinging kitchen doors before Charles could say anything else.

Esme was immediately drawn to the platters of Christmas biscuits covering the long kitchen counters, then sent her most winning look at Mrs Renwick. 'Yum. How many may I take?'

Mrs Renwick gave Esme her loving equivalent of a glare and placed yet another tray of perfect Christmas biscuits on the marble countertop. 'One. The rest are for the baskets I'm making up for the Christmas market.'

'Which ones are these again?' Esme reached out to take one of the little pink cloud-like treats, only to have her hand lightly slapped away.

'You know perfectly well they're peppermint divinity, Esme. Heaven knows, you've eaten enough of them each and every Christmas.' Esme dodged another tray of hot biscuits. 'Off you go. I'm busy here. Scoot.'

'Why can't I stay here with you?'

'Because you must have far better things to do than watch me mass-produce my Christmas biscuits.'

True, but…also…false. Nothing was holding her interest. Ever since Max had returned and *not* hunted her down, she'd felt listless. She took a biscuit and watched Mrs Renwick at work.

After a few minutes of being stared at, her honorary aunt gave an exasperated sigh. 'Esme Ross-Wylde, you are underfoot. Why don't you go to the lounge and talk to some of the residents?'

'Ha! No thank you.'

Mrs Renwick gave her a sidelong glance. 'You like seeing the residents.'

'That's true.' She took another biscuit. She did like spending time with them. Honestly, she did, it was just that *he* was out there and as he'd avoided her when he'd come back he obviously didn't want to talk to her. Then again, what if he thought *she* was avoiding *him*?

This was ridiculous. What was she? Twelve? There was no way she was going to get through the rest of the week unless they resolved the whole tension thing. But how?

It wasn't as if she was going to saunter up to him and say, *Hey, Max! Just so you know— I've got loads of trust and confidence issues thanks to my ex-husband. We got married when I was nineteen. I know...young, right? Anyway, I was grieving after my brother's death at the time, and the rest of the family were dealing with Nick's death in their own ways...you know how it is.*

One thing led to another—we eloped, he stole half of my trust fund and set up a night-club, but made it seem like I was reneging on my promise to set up a canine therapy cen-tre I'd told the universe I was going to estab-lish in honour of Nick's death. Yeah. I know! Not very nice. It makes a girl paranoid. So, anyway...the thing is... I'm really attracted to you and it freaks me out. So sorry if I'm being weird. Friends?

Yeah, that definitely wasn't going to happen.

Maybe she should bring a thank-you present for everything he'd done today. She scanned the kitchen. 'Is there anything I could take out to the residents as a night-time nibble?'

Mrs Renwick picked up a gloriously over-the-top chocolate cake. 'Here. Take this and leave me in peace.'

'Perfect.' She leant in and gave Mrs Renwick a kiss. 'Thank you, Christmas Fairy!'

When she left the kitchen the first person she laid eyes on was Max. He was at the doorway to the media room, staring intently at something. She poked her head in to see what was so interesting.

'Wow.'

Euan and Andy were playing some sort of scuba-diving treasure-hunt game, their two dogs curled up beside their armchairs. It looked as though the forty-something soldier and the twelve-year-old had been friends for life. Playing. Cheering one another on. It was all quiet and modulated, but…there was a kinship there. Two broken souls finding a safe place to be happy.

Sensing her rather than looking at her, Max said, 'This definitely falls into the category of things I thought I'd never see.'

'You're not wrong,' Esme agreed. 'I never thought I'd see Andy this interactive again.'

Max shot the pair a nervous look. 'Should I get Euan out of there?'

'No. Not at all, it's just…' She rested her head against the doorframe and watched the ex-soldier offer gentle instructions to Euan as he navigated the game. A splashing sound came out of the speaker and they both flinched. Then fist bumped each other. 'They've both found someone who understands what they're going through.'

Max nodded, his eyes still on the pair. 'They've each got PTSD for fairly different reasons, though.'

Esme's heart softened. This definitely wasn't virgin territory for him. 'I guess you know a fair few soldiers who came back from their tours seeing the world through a different lens.'

He scrubbed his hand along his jaw before answering. 'Everyone comes back from a conflict zone seeing the world differently.'

Not an insight exactly, but…she supposed she'd seen Glasgow as her 'conflict zone' after everything had gone wrong with Harding. It made hiding out up here too easy. Maybe it was time to see about that satellite clinic she kept promising herself she'd open one day.

They watched for a few moments as the game progressed. There was a third unused console sitting on a footstool. Esme pointed at it.

'You not playing?'

'Nah.' He shook his head, loosening those loose curls on top of his forehead again. 'I'm no good at fantasy.'

Oh, she would've bet actual money that he was very good at fulfilling fantasies.

Esme! Stop it. Your mind is very, very naughty. Especially when she was within a ten-foot radius of Mr Tall, Dark and Scrumptious here.

She shifted her weight to her other hip and balanced the cake on her left hand.

'After seeing you in action today, I would've thought you'd be good at anything you set your mind to.'

Uh-oh. That had come out more flirtatiously than she'd anticipated. Mostly because her eyes were on the same level as that yummy-looking mouth of his.

Her tooth caught her lower lip as she felt Max's dark eyes glint then take a leisurely inspection of her. Nice and slow from her hair, to her eyes, to her lips, to her…

'You always walk around your castle with a chocolate cake?'

'Yes.' She gave him a goody-goody smile. 'It's my evening ritual. It's required actually.'

'Oh?' That increasingly familiar little hitch of his eyebrow let her know he was back in flirt mode.

'Yes, that's right. Cake-bearing duties are obligatory for poor, beleaguered Highland spinsters who rely on their big brother's largesse for a roof over their heads.'

He snorted. Rightly so.

She had inherited plenty of money when her father had died. The trust fund thing had been awful, but her father had been clever enough not to give his children access to vast lump sums. Charles had inherited the castle in line with tradition, but it wasn't exactly as if he was pushing her out the front door. Quite the opposite, in fact. Both of them loved it here, but they would've traded it all if they could have had their brother back. It was one of the reasons Charles had suggested they turn it into a clinic. A way for them to work together, honour their brother, and make their home a place to heal.

Max's eyes dropped to the cake again. 'Are you planning on sharing any of that, or are you just going to walk round and show people what they aren't getting?'

The atmosphere between them went taut. Max wasn't talking about cake. Margaret's words coquettishly danced to the fore: *'What's the worst that could happen?'*

She was safe here. This was her home. She wasn't going to elope and give him all the PIN numbers to her bank accounts. Apart from that, Max Kirkpatrick simply didn't seem the type of man who would have any dealings with lies and deceit.

A mad urge to go with her gut instinct seized her. She swooped her finger into the thick icing then stuck the whorl of buttercream into her mouth, making a show of enjoying the rich icing as it melted on her tongue. 'Mmm...'

'Looks good.' Max's voice was as rough as his stubble. Not that she'd touched it. Yet. When she finished the icing she reached out to touch his cheek. He grabbed her wrist and swept her finger through the chocolate buttercream for a second time. 'Uh-uh.' He said. 'My turn.'

Esme's insides turned as hot as lava as he pulled her finger towards his mouth. *Oh, mercy.* He was going to— *Oh*...he did… He drew her finger into his mouth. It was hot and wet, and his tongue was making short work of that icing, but his eyes had not as much as blinked. This had to be one of the sexiest things that had ever happened to her and they were both completely clothed. She dreaded to think what would happen if they were naked.

No, she didn't. And that was a problem. She didn't dread it at all.

Just then Wylie bumbled over and gave her a nudge.

Max let go of her wrist.

'Your bodyguard?'

'Something like that.' Gulp. 'Want a proper slice?' She raised the cake.

'No.' He shook his head, his voice still thick with whatever it was that had just happened between them. 'Not hungry.'

'Neither am I.'

'Give it to the lads.'

'Okay.'

And just like that Esme walked into the media room, handed the video-game players the cake and two forks then walked straight back out again.

'Want to see my Christmas tree?' she asked Max.

'Is that a euphemism?'

'No. But it can be if you'd like it to be.'

Much to her astonishment, Max followed her as she silently led him towards the small sitting room in her and Charles's private wing. This, she was beginning to realise, was going to be a very different Christmas indeed.

CHAPTER SIX

'THIS DOOR HAVE a lock?'

Max knew they were in the private wing, but private also included Esme's older brother and the last thing he wanted was to get a black eye as a result of what he was about to do.

'No.' Esme swallowed. 'But my bedroom does.'

'So does mine.'

'Mine has mistletoe.'

'I don't need a reason to kiss you.' He smiled at her shocked expression. Finally! He'd called a spade a spade and put that humming buzzy friction crackling between them out in the open. He wanted her. She wanted him. The only question was where. 'Is Dougal in your room or mine?'

'He's in mine with Wylie. I think they're brand-new BFFs.' She held out her hand. 'Let's go to yours.'

He took her hand but didn't move anywhere. Instead he pulled her to him and did
what he'd wanted to do since that first moment he'd laid eyes on her. Cupped that perfect chin of hers between his thumb and
forefinger, tipped it up and kissed her. She
was every bit as sweet, hot and delicious as
he'd imagined.

When she parted her lips and their kisses
deepened, he felt things happening inside him
he definitely didn't want her big brother to
see.

'My room,' he rumbled. 'Now.'

She didn't need telling twice.

Moments later they were in the room, lock-
ing the door and tearing each other's clothes
off. Kissing as if their lives depended on it.
His top first. Her jumper next…a bit of a
stall as he relished the sensation of touching
that creamy, freckly, décolletage of hers. His
hands skimmed over the very nice lace of her
bra and he was rewarded with a moan as her
nipples turned into tight nibs under his touch.

Her skin was every bit as soft as he'd imagined. Staying steady and in control was almost impossible. In true 'everything's magic

at Heatherglen' style, someone had already been in and lit the fire in his room so enjoying the bit-by-bit exposure of Esme by firelight was little short of heaven.

'Let's slow it down,' he said when Esme started fiddling with his belt buckle.

She instantly froze beneath his hands. 'What? Why?'

He smiled at her aggrieved expression. 'I was just saying we have plenty of time—twelve days before Christmas.'

'It's seven, actually.' He could see her begin to withdraw emotionally. 'So...you don't want to do this?'

'Quite the opposite, darlin'. I've wanted you from the moment I laid eyes on you.' He dropped kisses on her forehead, her nose, her lips then said, 'The way I see it, once we start, there's no turning back. So we either agree that this is something that won't affect our "day jobs" while we're here or we walk away now.'

Esme actually whimpered. Which was just about the sweetest thing he'd ever heard. 'I don't want to walk away...'

'There's a lot you don't know about me.' A

lot he didn't want her to know. He'd been trying to leave the angry guy from the past behind for a long time now and he thought he'd finally done it, but…this whole business with Plants to Paws had dug up a bunch of unresolved feelings. Something about Esme made him want to wrap them up once and for all.

'Well…' Esme traced the pad of her fingertip along the stubble above his upper lip '…there's definitely a lot you don't know about me.' Her eyes provocatively flicked to his. 'But it doesn't seem to have stopped us from liking each other.'

As her finger traced round his lips then dipped into his mouth, he couldn't resist drawing it in deeper and giving it another swirl as if it were still slathered in chocolate icing. When he let go of it, he said, 'That's very true. Maybe we could call this getting-to-know-you time?'

'We could do that…'

He ran his thumb along the bare swoop of her waist to her hip and watched a smattering of goose pimples shift along her belly just as he'd thought they might. 'Am I sensing there is another part to that sentence?'

* * *

Esme had a choice here. She could tell Max the truth. Tell him she was scared. Scared of being betrayed. Of being taken advantage of. Of not being enough.

She could also tell him she was so ready to rip the rest of his clothes off she could hardly see straight. An urge she hadn't felt in years.

And yet here she was, standing in his arms with nothing on but her bra and her skirt while he was still mostly clothed. Which was strangely sexy. No. Not strangely at all. Everything about Max Kirkpatrick was sexy. The touch of his hands. The warmth of his skin. The way his eyes looked at her like she was the most beautiful thing he'd ever seen.

Max deserved an honest answer. One that she could live with, too.

She flattened her hand against his chest, just itching to tease her fingers through the sparse whorls of dark hair around his nipples, but stopped herself. Teasing him when she hadn't yet said yes was little short of cruel. To both of them.

She waited until she could feel the beat of his heart beneath her palm. It was fast. He was as nervous as she was. And as excited. She could tell that easily enough by leaning into him. Cotton trousers didn't hide much in the way of male arousal. Before she shifted her hand down and felt it, she had to make a decision.

He wasn't Harding MacMillan. Or any of the exceedingly bland men she'd dated to avoid heartbreak since. Max Kirkpatrick was one of a kind. Something deep within her told her he wanted nothing from her apart from honesty and respect. All of which spoke to the very essence of who she was. The fundamental spirit of how she wanted to live her life. Courageously. Openly. Honestly. Would this be her chance to restore that bright flame of confidence, which she'd once felt, flickering in her heart again?

She tilted her head up for another kiss. He saw the questions in her eyes and knew it would be the deciding factor. The kiss he gave in response told her all she wanted to know. It was everything she'd ever wanted in a kiss and more. Soft then responsive. Inquisitive. Passionate. Hungry. Wanting absolutely nothing of her but that she enjoy his touch.

Could she handle seven perfect days of Max and then watch him walk away?

When he shifted both his hands to her waist her goose pimples turned her insides to liquid gold. She pressed up against him so that her hips were just below his. 'Yes,' she said. 'If we keep it low key with the staff, I'd be grateful, but other than that? Let's dispense with the seven swans aswimming.'

Max didn't need any more encouragement. He swept his hands along her bottom, down to her thighs, and pulled her up so that her legs circled his hips so quickly she hardly had a chance to catch her breath. Didn't care if she did. She was already light-headed with her decision to give herself to this man. He was half untamed wild man, half cultured Casanova.

The light stubble on his cheeks brushed against her cheek as he carried her to his huge four-poster bed then laid her down on the thick linen bedding. She almost purred in response. Rough with the smooth. That was life, wasn't it? That was Max.

'It's a very nice room.' Max said, thinking she was cooing about the bedding.

'It's much nicer with you in it.'

A rakish smile crept onto his lips. 'Did you put me here by accident or design?'

'Neither,' she said with an innocent smile. 'Dr Sinclair does the room assignments. He thought you were going to be a thirty-something single mum. When he heard you were ex-military he said I'd be as safe as houses.'

'Is that what he told you?' His eyes lit up with a dangerously scrumptious glint.

'That's what he assumed.'

'Shall I show you what you can do with his assumptions?' Max began undoing his belt buckle.

'Yes, please.'

What followed was by turns heartfelt, carnal and utterly luxurious.

Max had never experienced lovemaking like this before. It felt by turns entirely new and utterly familiar. As if he'd been waiting his whole life to find this. To find her. To hold Esme in his arms. Not that she lay still long enough for him to give her a cuddle. No, she was busy exploring his body as if she'd found

Atlantis itself. He didn't mind being a stand-in for the mythical place. Not by a long shot.

She was busy tracing his abdomen at the moment. With her tongue. By the time she hit that divot between his ribcage and his hips, her blonde hair tickling the wake of where her hot, wet mouth had just been, he wanted nothing more than to turn the tables. It was his turn to pleasure her. Tease every tiny moan and groan of which she was capable out of her. Bring her to the climax he could already sense building inside her.

Before she could dip any lower, he pulled her into his arms and flipped her onto her back, her hair splayed out around her like a halo, her blue eyes glistening in the firelight. 'Now it's your turn.'

As she had earlier, she pressed her palm to his chest as if to bond their hearts. When she was satisfied that the beat of his own heart matched hers, he kissed her so hard and with such depth of emotion he could have disappeared into the kiss and never come back again. From the intensity of her response, she was feeling the same way.

After an utterly decadent spell of exploring her body he was barely containing his own heated tension. When she arched into the taut length of him it was all he could do not to thrust himself deep inside her and find his climax. It would come easily and quickly, as he suspected hers would as well. But he didn't want that for Esme. He wanted slow, and intense and meaningful. Then maybe another round that was hot and fast. Yet another that was dirty and dangerous. And then they could spend the rest of the time they had left figuring out all the other ways the two of them made sense.

As if reading his mind, she smiled at him with such desire in her eyes he felt his heart seem to nearly double in size. Quadruple. Whatever. All he knew was that he cared about her. Knowing she felt the same way was worth its weight in gold. There was something vulnerable about her he wanted to protect. Something fiery in her, brave even, that he wanted to nurture. Though they had come from different worlds, he felt he knew her and that with each passing day there would be discoveries that would only make knowing her even more enriching than it already had been. So long as he didn't do anything stupid like fall in love—

'Stop thinking.' Esme held his face between her hands. 'I want you inside me.'

This was the one time in his life he felt utterly obliged to do as the lady wished.

After a scramble for protection and an intensely pleasurable few moments ignoring Esme's cries for him to stop what he was doing with his fingers because she couldn't hold back much longer, Max was certain she wanted him as much as he wanted her. He positioned himself so that the thick tautness of his desire finally dipped between her legs. Her hips were urging him to enter her. He somehow managed to exhibit a bit more restraint than Esme, who was virtually glittering with frustrated desire under him. When at long last he finished teasing her, he pushed inside her. Both of them groaned with pleasure. If there'd been any doubt before, it was a certainty now. They were made for each other. Their bodies moved in a synchronicity he had never experienced before. An undulating cadence that built and strengthened and empowered.

He wanted to let loose. He wanted her to feel him completely inside her. He wanted to bring her to a climax she would never forget.

'Do it,' she whispered. 'Take me.'

There was absolutely no hesitancy or fear in her voice. Only pure, undiluted desire.

He did as she bid.

When the moment of fulfilment came Esme cried out his name and Max actually saw stars. He almost laughed. If he told Esme she'd insist it was a Christmas star. He'd tell her sometime why it was such a complicated day for him. But for now he just wanted to hold his slightly breathless, incredibly beautiful, Christmas angel in his arms. That was more than enough Christmas magic for him.

Esme would've happily stayed snuggled all warm and cosy in Max's arms for the rest of the day. Longer if her tummy wasn't rumbling. Thank goodness he was still asleep and couldn't hear all of her mere mortal noises because last night…last night had been straight out of the heavenly bodies notebook. He was right. Once they'd had a taste of what intimacy was like between the pair of them? Catnip. Once hadn't been enough. Or twice. It was like discovering herself all over again. Discovering just how magical a connection between two people could be had been little short of revelatory. If not a tiny bit scary. He was perfect. And she was scared of perfect because she'd thought she'd had perfect once before and how wrong she'd been.

Even so, something told her she had to find a way to start trusting her instincts again. It had been over ten years since Harding had well and truly pulled the wool over her eyes. Surely she'd learnt her lesson by now. If what her gut was telling her was true, Max was the real deal. Complex. Loving. Generous, sharing, caring, sensual. She gave his hand, which she'd been using as a mini-pillow, a kiss. Yes, he was all that and more. The big, strong soldier was vividly on show every time he scooped her up and flipped her this way or that on the bed. But there was also a tender, unbelievably sensitive man whose hands could… Ooh…goosebumps.

When her phone alarm went off before the sun had even thought about coming up, she was tempted to throw it out the window, but duty called. Max's hand reached out to bat at the snooze button, but she swatted it away and turned the alarm off. 'Uh-uh. Sorry, pal. I've got a long day of surgery ahead.'

'Surgery?'

'Yup.' She rolled over so she could face him, pulling a sheet up to her mouth in case she had morning breath.

'What are you doing?'

'Hiding my morning breath from you. Hey. Stop that! Don't. OMG, what if I kill you with morning breath?'

Max made a big stagey inhalation then grinned. 'Delicious. Just like a candy cane. Now, out with it. What's with the surgery?'

She grinned, pleased that he was interested, and sat up, pulling a swirl of sheet around her as she did so. 'Well! I have a knee surgery for a Great Dane.'

'Sounds interesting.'

'It will be. It's an ACL surgery. Almost identical to the ones they do for top athletes.'

He arced an eyebrow. 'Cruciate ligament on a giant breed. Definitely interesting. Can I tag along?'

Her eyebrows scrunched together. 'Don't you want to be with Euan for his training?'

He gave his jaw a scrub. 'They're going on some sort of outing today with Margaret. To a shopping centre, I think. I've noticed Euan tends to defer to me when he's nervous about something and seeing that he and I aren't going to be attached at the hip when we get back to Glasgow, I was wondering what you thought about the idea of letting him get on with things?'

Esme leant in and gave him a soft kiss. Margaret hadn't needed to farm him out for babysitting. He'd been well aware of what had been going on all along. 'You're much sweeter in real life than you let on.'

He growled and pounced on her until they were a kissing, cuddling, giggling tangle of legs, arms and duvet. When they flopped back onto the pillows with a contented sigh, Esme reluctantly climbed out of bed.

'Right! I'd better get across the hall before my brother sees me do the walk of shame.'

Max jiggled his eyebrows. 'Is this a frequent occurrence?

'Pah! Hardly.' Like never. 'Not even close.

But he'd probably have a heart attack if he saw me tiptoeing out of a man's room. After last time—'

She clapped her hands to her mouth.

He traced a line from her throat to the little divot between her shoulder blades. 'Want to talk about it?'

She didn't. But as she'd actively avoided talking about her past to every single man she'd ever dated before, perhaps it was time to see what happened if she was as open and honest as she wanted the men in her life to be.

'Later?'

'How about after work? I'll pick you up at yours.' He winked. She blushed. It was settled.

She was going to have a date to discuss her evil ex-husband with her lover and it felt like the right thing to do.

She gave his hand another kiss. 'Sounds good.' She quickly pulled on her clothes for the run down the corridor.

'You're sure you're cool with me watching you in surgery today?'

'Why wouldn't I be? You watched yesterday.'

'Yesterday I hadn't seen you naked.'

'Good point.' It wasn't very fun thinking of what lay ahead when all she wanted to concentrate on was the here and now, but… 'Not to throw ice on this or anything, but I do live and work here. As you'll be leaving in a week, maybe we'd be best keeping it quiet?'

'Sounds sensible. Your wish is my command.'

Oh! That was easy. There were a thousand ways he could've responded to her request to keep things quiet, but the way Max had taken on board what she'd said made her feel as though she'd really been listened to. Maybe this was what adult relationships were like. Honest. Straightforward. And super sexy.

Max pulled her in close so that she was standing between his legs as he sat on the edge of the bed. Mmm… He smelt of warm bedding and cloves and some sort of special man scent. *Yum.*

He pulled her in for a kiss then held her a few inches back and spoke in an exaggerated brogue. 'All right, then, ma wee lassie. Just be warned, if anyone tries to swoop in and claim you, I'll tilt my lance for ye.'

Swoon!

If she didn't watch herself, it would be very, very easy to fall for this man.

'Excellent. I shall get Wylie to do the same on my behalf.' She was quite sure the St Bernard would know how to keep other women at bay. Slobber them to death most likely. 'Speaking of that, I'd better let poor Dougal out. He and Wylie need a quick spin round the block before I head off to the clinic. Interested?'

He shook his head. 'I've got a few phone calls to make to the Clyde and I'll have breakfast with Euan as I'll be abandoning him all day.'

He pulled her in for a final kiss and when they finally came up for air she knew she'd have a big challenge ahead of her in regard to keeping this romance under the radar. Hiding the way she felt about him would be little short of impossible.

CHAPTER SEVEN

EVEN WITH HER entire body buzzing from the last twenty-four hours, Esme was not going to be kept from her morning cup of coffee. She was in the middle of frothing up some milk when Margaret walked into the staff-room with the daily schedule.

One look at Esme was all it took. 'Ooh! I see why you blew me off last night.'

Esme's plan to not tell anyone lasted about two seconds before she cracked. 'It wasn't strictly planned but...' Her smile stretched from ear to ear.

'Finally.' Margaret accepted the proffered latte and took a big slurp before giving Esme's arm a congratulatory pat. 'I was going to have to reclassify you as a virgin if you hadn't got some action soon.'

'Crickey.' Esme play-sulked because she was too happy to actually sulk. 'I didn't think I was that dire a case.'

Margaret rolled her eyes. 'Oh, believe me, Ez. You were definitely on the brink of being sent to a nunnery.' She shot a surreptitious look out the door towards the main reception area. 'So what is he? Short term or long term?'

Her gut said long term. Her head told her otherwise. 'Short terms. Obviously.'

'Why obviously? He's hot. And you look all loved up, so…if it works, why cut it short?'

'Cut what short?' Max appeared in the doorway. 'Sorry, ladies. Was I interrupting something?'

'No!' they both shouted, then burst into giggles, which, of course, answered his question.

Esme choked out something about coffee, which Max accepted with a bemused grin. She busied herself making the coffee, praying he wasn't noticing Margaret's eyes ping-ponging between the pair of them as if she was expecting cartoon love hearts to blossom out of thin air and float round the staffroom. She wasn't *that* loved up.

Max took the cup of coffee from her and when their fingers brushed, she blushed.

Okay. Maybe she had a *crush* on him. Big

time. But that was normal when a girl had had such a lengthy hiatus from romance. A Christmas dalliance, she reminded herself when her eyes travelled across the room to the mistletoe hanging in the doorway.

Margaret took another big slurp of her coffee then asked, 'Shall I run you through what I'm doing with Euan and Fenella today before I leave you two lovebirds to it?'

Max choked on his coffee. Esme's cheeks flamed.

'That would be lovely, Margaret.' Esme had her public-school voice back on. 'Please. Do tell us.'

With an unapologetic grin, Margaret launched into a detailed explanation of the trip they'd be taking to the shopping mall, where Euan in particular would have a chance to deal with the loud noises. They'd work with how the dog could help in stressful situations. 'It's getting so close to Christmas it's going to be very busy.'

'Six days,' Esme said, a bit too aware of the countdown to Christmas.

Max gave a little involuntary shudder. 'You sure you're all right with the pair of them on their own? It might be a lot for Euan to take on board.'

'He needs to get used to dealing with these things and if we ease him in with these baby steps, it'll be much more useful once you get back to Glasgow.' She pulled her mobile out of her pocket. 'I've got one of these and know the staff at the shopping centre well, so if there are any problems I'll give you a tinkle. You two enjoy yourselves in surgery.'

'Oh, we plan to,' Max said, rubbing his hands together.

'I'll bet you do,' Margaret said, then swished out of the room.

Esme shook her head. For heaven's sake! So, she'd had sex. No need to make a song and dance out of the whole thing. She glanced at the clock on the wall to gauge just how much time they had before her first dog came in for surgery.

Max looked at Esme as her smile widened. 'What?'

A few hours in, Max had to admit that watching Esme at work was on a par with observing the finest surgeons at work in war zones.

He'd never thought veterinarians were less skilled than human doctors, quite the opposite in fact, but he'd never really taken on board how much more complex it was because her patients couldn't explain where it hurt.

Didn't seem to matter to Esme. She appeared to have a sixth sense about them. And their owners. She was focused, exacting and utterly intent on bringing about the best results for her patient. After Max had popped on a set of the clinic's scrubs and a fleece, he parked himself in the corner as Esme kicked off the day with the promised cruciate ligament surgery for Arthur, a Great Dane who was virtually eye to eye with Esme when standing. Which wasn't long, because she liked to keep their distress to a minimum.

After Arthur's rather astonishing surgery, she neutered a cat and a dog, removed a large growth from a chocolate Labrador's spleen, sewing him up with the same exacting stitches she'd exhibited on Teasel, and plucked a rather painful-looking thorn from a bloodhound's paw without eliciting as much as a whimper of discomfort from the dog.

This, on top of an emergency extraction of a chicken bone stuck in a Chihuahua's throat, operating on a bulldog's cherry eye whilst singing 'Rudolph the Red Nosed Reindeer', much to the delight of the vet nurses, and taking off the bandages and pronouncing good health to a ferret who had suffered a serious cut after getting stuck in a bit of guttering.

Unlike most of the human surgeons he'd met, she was also completely soppy. And not just with puppies. Any animal that entered her exam room or surgery brought that soft, dewy-eyed expression to her face as if she'd never before seen anything so utterly adorable. No wonder their patient roster was filled to bursting. All the pet owners absolutely adored her!

The bell tinkled above the main door to Reception just as Esme was dropping off a prescription for an arthritic lurcher. A woman wearing riding clothes, including her helmet, rushed in, carrying a heavy cardboard box. 'Help! Please! Can you help!'

'Mrs McCann? What's happened?'

'It's Honeybear!' wailed the ashen faced woman.

Esme rushed over to her side to help her, her entire body stilling as she saw what was inside. 'Max?' She threw him a quick look. 'Could you do us a favour?'

He came over and looked inside. It was a smallish dog—a beagle—who looked as though it had been hit by a car. He was alive, but bleeding from a bad cut on his right hip, and was panting in clear distress.

'Would you mind bringing Honeybear back to the surgical room? I'll be right behind you.' He heard her ask the nursing staff to get the woman a cup of sweet tea and to see if they could call Aksel to come in a bit earlier than the afternoon shift they had him scheduled for. She also asked them to ring Arthur the Great Dane's owners and tell them he was doing just fine in Recovery and could be collected at the end of the day.

The second she was in surgery she was a picture of undeterred focus. Surgical cap, gown and mask on. Her instructions were crisp, thoughtful and modulated. Every single member of her team was made to feel like that…a member of a team. Which was every bit as sexy as Esme naked in his bed.

He liked a confident woman. He liked Esme. More and more as the day progressed. All of which meant saying goodbye come Christmas Eve was going to be a wrench, but… He stuffed the thoughts away. No need to think about it now.

'You don't have to stand back if you don't want to.' Esme smiled across at him. 'Since you brought her in, you're part of the team. If you scrub in, you can come on over to the table and see how the real doctors do it!' She dropped him a wink. 'All right, Honeybear, let's get you on the table, shall we?' Deftly she inserted an IV drip into the front paw one of her nurses had just shaved. They also fitted an oxygen mask to her small muzzle. 'Lainey? Can we please get some samples?'

'What are those for?' Max asked from the scrub sink in the adjacent room. Nothing was going to stop him from being a part of this.

Esme worked as she spoke. 'We need to see what the packed cell volume is, total solids, glucose and BUN.'

'Same as for humans? The BUN levels?' Max asked.

'Exactly. Dogs need kidneys every bit as

much as humans. If this little chap's kidneys can't remove urea from the blood, the same things happen to him as happen to a human.'

She didn't need to spell it out. It was bad. The critical diagnostic test would indicate whether or not they needed to worry about liver damage, urinary tract obstruction or even gastrointestinal bleeding.

'The IV includes painkiller as well as fluids,' Esme explained. 'Apparently he was running alongside Mrs McCann when she was out for her daily ride on Hercules.'

'And he is...?'

'Her shire horse. She likes to go for a bit of a hack through the woods up here on the estate but something spooked him and he kicked out. Unfortunately, Honeybear was caught, the poor wee thing. It's all right,' she cooed at the dog, who was beginning to feel the effects of the sedative she'd just given him. 'All right, darling.' She grabbed a pair of scissors and a stack of swabs. 'Let's see what's going on in here, shall we?'

Half an hour and a set of X-rays later, the prognosis was better than expected.

'What would your assessment be, Dr Kirkpatrick?'

Max had been so absorbed in the examination he answered instantly. 'Initial observations are to keep an eye on the laceration on his right hip, presumably from the horseshoe. Perhaps the horse's hoof should be checked. There might be a loose nail in there judging by the jagged edge of the cut. I would give Honeybear a tetanus shot if they aren't up to date. His pelvic fracture will need external stabilisation. It doesn't appear to be displaced, but...' He glanced at the X-rays hanging on the wall again.

'If he were a patient in my ER, I would advise one or two days in hospital to stabilise. He'll need monitoring because of the damage and swelling. There's always the possibility that there's some internal bleeding we haven't caught yet.' He wove his fingers together on top of his head as he leant in for a closer look. 'The blunt trauma of the injury will cause significant bruising and swelling so any chance of haematomas or clotting will need to be reduced.'

Esme nodded, only her bright blue eyes visible above her mask.

'So…you wouldn't put him down despite the catastrophic injuries?'

Max stood bolt upright. 'No. You wouldn't do that to a human! Put them down just because of a bit of recovery time.'

Soft little fans of crinkles appeared at the sides of Esme's eyes. 'Very good, Doctor. A few more years of university and you'd make an excellent veterinarian here at the CTC if you ever decided to change over.' The soft, approving look he knew was just for him sparkled with delight, then abruptly shifted back into professional mode as there were about four other staff members waiting for Honeybear's actual assessment.

'He'll definitely need a bit of time to recover from the shock before we do anything other than make sure this cut doesn't bleed any more. The only other thing is that once the swelling goes down, the pelvic fracture could require stabilising surgery rather than observed cage rest. Although… I agree. If we can avoid surgery, it'd be better for this little one. Possibly seven to ten days' cage rest would do the trick, which would mean…' Her eyes flicked across at a large digital clock and calendar. 'It would mean, if all goes well, you just might be home in time for Christmas with your mum! It's what everyone wants, isn't it? To be home for Christmas with their loved ones?' Her eyes flicked to Max's just in time to catch his inevitable wince.

He felt awful. She wasn't to know his stepdad used to make Christmas the unhappiest time of year. From day one Max had never able to put a foot right in his stepdad's immaculate home. Or say the right thing. Or give the right presents. So much so the frequently made suggestions that he stay behind at the military academy to make sure he was on top of his studies had soon become the easiest option to keep his mum out of an ever-increasing line of verbal fire.

When she shot him an *Are you okay?* look, he excused himself. There was a side door out to a small covered porch just outside the surgical ward. He tugged on a gilet and went out into the wintry air and sucked in a deep breath. He cursed himself under his breath. He couldn't help feeling like that twelve-year-old boy who'd wanted nothing more than his stepfather's love. The eighteen-year-old boy intent on hating everything about him. The man who *bah-humbugged* his way through Christmas just to keep the dark memories at bay.

Time to grow up. Flinching and wincing and bracing himself against any and all things Christmas didn't change a damn thing. He looked in the window to the room leading to the operating theatre and saw Esme carefully carrying Honeybear in her arms, deftly shifting him into one of the fleece-lined kennels. His heart squeezed so tightly he could barely breathe, and he knew it wasn't the north wind that was making it so.

Perhaps he'd reached a crossroads. A point where he had to stop withdrawing from life, from relationships, friendships even for fear of messing them up. Sure, he'd taken a step into more intimate territory with Esme, but there was an automatic expiry date built into that. December the twenty-third—the night of the ball.

He barked out a laugh. Trust him to make

sure he didn't have anything good to look forward to on Christmas Day.

He didn't have an immediate solution for the Christmas problem, but he knew it was time to change how he thought about relationships. Which meant moving on from that boy desperate for love. The young soldier intent on proving he was worth the wait, only to find out his efforts had been for naught. He wanted to open his heart to Esme. It wasn't right to keep her at arm's length, as he had everyone else in his adult life. What was the worst that could happen? His heart might break a little? Maybe this time the pain would be worth it.

He looked back at exactly the same moment as Esme crossed to the window, presumably to look for him. When she saw him her face lit up, her forehead lightly furrowed with concern. She put her hand up to the window. He reached out and pressed his to meet hers. When their eyes met? Magic.

Yes. She was worth the risk all right. Worth that and then some. Bring it on, Christmas. This A and E doc was ready to get his jingle on.

* * *

The last patient of the day was a very poorly Pomeranian called Snowy, who had stolen a mince pie off her owner's kitchen table. A quick injection to clear her stomach did the trick. Not very nice for poor old Snowy, but Max, much to Esme's amusement, had the giggles.

'This the sort of thing that tickles your funny bone?' she asked.

'No, sorry.' He tried to wipe that adorable smirk from his face and couldn't. Which, of course, made her laugh.

Esme gave Snowy an apologetic cuddle. The poor wee thing could've died from eating the mince pie, which was toxic to dogs. It was no laughing matter. She gave Max his next 'quiz' as he'd requested throughout the day. 'Any idea what comes next for this little one?'

'An IV for fluids and mild food like rice or scrambled eggs for the next couple of days?'

Esme beamed. 'Got it in one.' She held the little fluffy dog up in front of her and asked it, 'What on earth could be so funny about watching you get sick that made big old Dr Max have the giggles?'

All of which set Max off again. 'It reminds me of weekends at the Clyde. I know I shouldn't laugh. It's not funny. But at this time of year there is always someone at an office party who manages to overdo it and in they come and out *it* comes and…well…' He crossed over to Esme's side and gave the fluffy pooch a tender little scrub on the head. 'I'm glad there's a happy ending.'

A warm swirl of happiness shifted round Esme's heart as she watched Max's features soften. It was similar to the look he got whenever Euan texted him to say he and Ajax had aced something. He'd sent Max a selfie about an hour earlier from the shopping centre, surrounded by crowds. Euan's smile was bigger than he'd ever seen it. Max had been so proud he'd looked fit to burst. She wondered if he'd look even more proud if he had children of his own one day. A wife.

She swallowed down the thoughts because even considering putting a ring back on her finger was absolutely ludicrous. Particularly given the fact she was going to bare her soul to him tonight and whatever this was between them might very quickly become past tense. She'd thought of countless reasons to change her mind and every bit as many to stay on course. The smile on Max's face was one of them.

'All right, then! I'll get one of the nurses to set Snowy up with a drip.'

Half an hour later, after Esme had done a final round of checks on everyone, she and Max were the only ones left in the clinic. She pulled off her surgical cap, ran her hands through her hair and gave it a good old shake. 'Phew! What a day!'

Max was looking at her with an odd expression on his face.

'What? Do I have something on my face?'

'Nope.' He pulled her to him, hip to hip, her breasts brushing against that big man chest of his. 'Nothing but pure perfection.' He dipped his head down and gave her the slowest, softest, most sensual kiss she could bear without her body turning to complete jelly. When he finally pulled back, which was too soon, he dipped his forehead to hers. 'Mmm… I've been wanting to do that all day.'

Esme's butterflies swiftly adorned themselves with feather boas and started dancing to sexy music. 'Is there anything else you've been wanting to do all day?'

'There most definitely is, ma wee lassie.' Max's voice swept through her like wildfire. If there had been blinds to draw on the big glass entryway to the veterinary clinic she would have drawn them immediately and torn off his scrubs in record time. 'I think we should have pizza.'

Er... It wasn't entirely what she was expecting to hear but, okay. 'You're hungry?'

He circled his arms round her waist and leant back with a big grin on his face. 'Yup. And you must be too after a big day like that. Impressive stuff, Dr Ross-Wylde.'

Despite herself, she blushed. 'We tend not to go by "Doctor" in the veterinary world.'

'Well, you should. It's extraordinarily difficult to diagnose a patient who can't speak to you. I thought we played a bit of a guessing game in human diagnostics, but you take it to another level. Impressive.'

She play-punched him in the arm. Getting compliments for doing what she loved most was great. Getting them from Max was some seriously divine icing on top. Speaking of which… 'Fancy any more of that chocolate cake of Mrs Renwick's, if there's any left?'

She pressed close to him and felt his response to the naughty glint in her eye and the low purr of seduction in her voice. Who knew she could be a sex kitten? Who knew this would be the man to bring it out of her?

'Pizza first,' he said, though she could feel his arousal though his scrubs.

She kissed one of his nipples through his top. Then the other. 'Don't you want to take a hot shower first? Wash off the day and get ready for the rest of it?' She tried to slip her hands under his top to get better access to that scrummy chest of his. Windows be damned!

He held her out at arm's length. 'Compromise?'

'Depends on the compromise.' She wriggled in closer, unable to shut down the primitive need to feel the warmth of his body.

'You said you had something you wanted to share with me so I thought perhaps I should as well.'

The part of her that had zero confidence in

herself instantly wanted to shrink away but she forced herself to hold eye contact.

'Sounds a bit scary.'

He gave a light shrug and a soft smile. 'Not if you're eating pizza.'

She almost laughed. When he put it that way…

He held open the door for her and tilted his head towards the castle. 'I saw a wood-fired pizza van out by the Christmas carnival. Thought maybe we could get ourselves some and then tuck ourselves away somewhere warm to eat it.'

An idea struck.

'I know *exactly* where we should go.'

Max smiled and held out his hand towards the door. 'Right, then, m'lady. Lead the way.'

CHAPTER EIGHT

'IT WAS SWEET of Euan to offer to look after Dougal while we came up here,' Esme said as she climbed the stairs without as much as breaking a sweat.

'He's a good kid.' Max took a peek out of a window he was passing. Three stories and counting. 'This is an awful lot of stairs to climb for a pizza date.' Max wasn't complaining. But he was bewildered. 'Are you sure you've not put the dungeon at the top of the castle?'

'Ha! No. There *is* a dungeon in the old castle. A poor little girl was stuck in it the other week, but Cass and Lyle saved her.'

'Who's going to save us if we get stuck up here?' Max joked.

'My big brother,' she said brightly over her shoulder.

'Does he step in to save you from all your bad dates?'

The smile dropped from her face and she picked up her pace. 'Just a couple more flights to go.'

Well, that put him on ice. Or perhaps he'd just jumped the gun on the 'something she wanted to talk about'.

A couple of minutes later he and Esme were standing looking out over the whole of the Christmas carnival and beyond. It was a sparkling mass of light and laughter and... even he had to admit it...it was magical. They must've been a good four or five storeys up. Five, most likely as he could see the roofing of the rest of the castle alongside them. The room was small, octagonal and incredibly cosy. A deep cushioned bench seat had been built under the windows that ran around the room.

They were just about level with the star on the enormous Christmas tree at the centre of the carnival. To their right was the skating rink. Beyond that were the twinkling lights twisting through the maze with a miniature castle in the centre rising up as a goal for the happy carnival-goers. Snow was falling lightly. It was truly a winter wonderland.

'It's amazing, isn't it?' Esme whispered as she tucked herself onto the window seat. 'I used to sneak up here as a kid with Nick and Charles and we'd watch everyone on the skating rink.'

'Then you probably saw me one of those nights.'

She shook her head, still trying to reconcile the big, strong man beside her and the young boy who had come here with his mum. 'I wouldn't have thought something this Christmassy would have been your thing.' She was teasing, not accusing, so he decided to just go for it.

He sat down beside her and took one of her hands in his, both their eyes still trained on the scene. 'It was when I was twelve.'

Esme gave his hand a squeeze. 'Want to tell me about it?'

'Yes,' he said, surprised at the raw emotion in his voice. 'Yes, I do.'

Esme listened, wide-eyed, as Max told his story. She knew he must've had a rough childhood, but the more she heard the more her heart ached for him.

'And you didn't mind being a latchkey kid?'

Max shook his head. 'It was the only life I knew. Besides, we were happy, Mum and me.'

'Even though she worked all those crazy shifts at the factory?'

'Yup. She was pretty strict about what I was and wasn't allowed to do and, lucky her, I was one of those dorky kids who always wanted to make her happy.'

Esme swatted at the air between them. 'I can in no way imagine that you were ever a dorky kid.'

'Well…' he acquiesced. 'Maybe in the privacy of my own home. I had my tough-kid image to look after on the mean streets of Glasgow after all.'

'You weren't in a gang or anything like that?'

'No. But there were gangs and the last thing you could show was weakness. I was hardly going to brag to all the other kids that I knew how to roast a chicken and make Yorkshire puddings.'

'Wow!' Esme's eye pinged open. 'You can cook?'

'Had to if I wanted to eat. My mum used

to leave me recipes. You must have a huge kitchen here. What can you make?'

She shot him a bashful look. 'True confession? Mrs Renwick always did it so well and Mum wasn't all that interested, so I never really learnt.' Before he could reply she said, 'I suppose I could learn. I wonder how long it would take?'

Max laughed. 'If you're planning on replacing your job with a pinafore, please don't. I like you just the way you are.'

'Really?'

Max shot her an inquisitive look. 'Of course. You're an amazing woman. Anyone who thinks otherwise can jog on to the land of no return as far as I'm concerned.'

'Thank you. That means a lot.'

She hadn't meant to sound as bone-achingly grateful as she did, but... Harding Mac-Millan hadn't liked her just the way she had been. He'd liked the bells and whistles and had merely tolerated her as a means to an end.

Max picked up another piece of pizza, his gaze drifting back out to the wintry scene.

'What was so magical about the time you were here with your mum?'

'It was our last proper Christmas together.' The sentence came out harsh and blunt.

'Did she—did something happen to her?'

'She got married.'

'Isn't that normally a good thing?'

'It is if the man in question is after a twelve-year-old son.'

'Oh, Max.' Her heart squeezed so tight for him she could barely breathe. As a young boy who'd never known a father's love, it must've been complete torture. 'Did he not even try?'

Max tossed the remains of his slice of pizza into the box and closed the lid. Thinking about his stepdad clearly wasn't good for his appetite.

'I used to call him the Dictator.'

That didn't sound good. 'And now?'

She saw something flicker in his eyes. A moment's hesitation as if he were debating whether or not to tell her something. 'I call him Gavin Henshall.'

Everything in her stilled.

So this was what he'd wanted to tell her. He was using her to get back at someone.

'Is that why you agreed to accept my help?' There was no chance he didn't hear the wobble in her voice.

He scrubbed a hand through his hair, looked out the window then back to her. 'I should've told you that first day. It's been eating at me ever since.'

'Why didn't you?' She forced the roar of blood in her ears into submission. She'd shared a bed with this man. If she was going to find out she'd been a pawn in something, she at least wanted to hear why.

'Because it was so personal. As you've probably noticed, sharing what's in here...' he thumped a fist against his chest '...doesn't come easily. Gavin changed my life and not in a good way. My mum's, too. But I didn't want you to think I was after revenge when what I really wanted was to save Plants to Paws.'

Her hammering heart slowed its cadence. He was being honest. Looking her straight in the eye. If it was revenge he was after... well, he'd hardly be telling her now, would he? Before he'd seen as much as a penny. And then the proverbial penny dropped. He was telling her now because he didn't want her to find out later and with that revelation her heart opened far wider than she'd let it open in years. She knew how hard it was to separate rage and pain. She'd had her own fair share of teasing the two apart over the years and a castle to 'hide' in to do it. Max had literally been on the front line and despite the incalculable amount of good he'd done, she could now see it was his past that was tearing at his heart.

'Well.' Esme sniffed imperiously. 'If he isn't a very nice man, I'm doubly glad we're keeping Plants to Paws as it is.'

The relief in Max's eyes brought tears to her own.

'At the beginning, when he was courting my mum, he was all right. She'd made it very clear that we came as a package.' He huffed out a laugh as his eyes travelled back out to the skating rink. 'She used to date a man for at least six months before they were even allowed to meet me. Said she had to vet them to make sure they were top-grade father material. It made me think I was this special kid. Worth waiting for.' His unhappy tone made it clear that special was the last thing he'd been made to feel.

Esme bristled on his behalf. 'Every child should believe they're safe. Protected. Your mum sounds amazing. Not all single parents are so discerning.'

'Not all single parents met slimeballs like him.' There was no mistaking the bitterness in his voice now.

'Did he hurt you?'

He scrubbed his hands along his trousers as if trying to get rid of a bad feeling. 'No. But he used to… I think the term they use now is psychological abuse.'

'To you?'

'Mostly to my mum. Which killed me. Because I was powerless to do anything.'

'Why powerless?'

'He always had an answer or a comeback that I couldn't respond to. He was a master of manipulation. And he shipped me off to military academy as soon as he could.'

'How awful.'

He tilted his head to one side, as if weighing up whether her response was valid. When he lifted his eyes to meet hers his eyes burned with fury. 'It was. But not for the reasons you'd think.'

Esme pushed both pizza boxes away and wrapped her arms around her knees. She was desperate to throw them round Max but the last thing she thought he'd want was pity. He must have felt so helpless watching the person he loved most in the world fall prey to the man who had promised to look after her. Both of them. A Jekyll and Hyde from the sound of it. 'What sort of things did he do?'

'Before they were married, he promised her a house on the nice side of town and a chance to be a stay-at-home mum. Host dinner parties, tend the garden, which she loved, that sort of thing.'

'That doesn't sound too awful.'

'It is when everything comes with conditions.' His smile was grim. 'She didn't get a choice of which house or where. Who she hosted at her parties. Which types of foods she could make. The clothes she could wear. The topics she could discuss when she was allowed to talk.'

Ouch. Her own marriage had been a bit like that. Indulgent at first. Indulgent until there had been a ring on her finger. The fact Harding had managed to fool her seemed insane now but, in hindsight, they'd all been reeling from Nick's death and Harding had brought some focus to their lives. Something to look forward to. A wedding. Grandchildren. If only she'd known how devious his 'courtship' had actually been.

Harding, who laid claim to some mysterious title, had insisted they go to the *right* balls and the *proper* restaurants and be seen with the *best* people. The types of people who tended to travel with paparazzi in tow. He might've even tipped them off, for all she knew. She'd been so naive, sad and lonely down there in Glasgow, away from her family and so desperate to feel loved she'd gone along with it all.

If Max's mum had felt that way… She wrapped her arms even tighter round herself. The poor woman. The only blessing was she hadn't had the tabloids smearing her misery all over the front pages.

'Are you cold?' Max started to take off his fleece.

'No, just…' *Just reliving some of the worst*

memories of her life, that was all. 'Please. Go on.'

'Well, as I said, one of the first things he did to rip away any link to her old life was to pronounce me a bad seed in need of some proper schooling, so he sent me to a military academy.'

'Bad seed? The chicken roasting, Yorkshire pudding making latchkey kid was a bad seed?'

He shrugged. 'I could've hung out with a better crowd, but where we lived there weren't exactly choice pickings. It was all a bit rough and ready on our estate. In all honesty, military academy suited me. I got on pretty well there and I kept thinking that the better I did, the sooner I could come home and make sure Mum was all right. It was pre-mobile phone years for kids so I couldn't call home, wasn't sure if she got my letters. I was completely powerless.'

'You said he didn't hit her, right?'

'No, but he may as well have for all the damage he did. *Not...*' he held up his hands '...that I would ever, ever condone hitting someone. Or putting them down. Just as vi-

cious. Just as cruel. He was always pick-
ing on her. What she wore. How she set the
table. Belittling her in front of guests when
the whole time he was the one who was small
and insignificant.'

'Social climber?' she guessed.

His grim expression told her all she needed
to know.

'I'm so sorry you both had to go through
that. Did you get her out in the end?'

Much to her astonishment, Max's eyes
glassed over. She let him wrestle with his
emotions rather than pressing him to speak.
She knew the courage it took to admit something hadn't gone the way you'd wanted it
to. The core-deep fear she'd felt when she'd
finally told her father what her ex-husband
had done had been the scariest, most isolat-
ing sensation she'd ever experienced.

The love and unconditional response she'd
received in return had set the bar high. Too
high, some might say, but…waiting for someone who would love her that unconditionally
was critical. She reached out and took one of
Max's hands in both of hers. She pressed her

cheek to the back of it then gave it a soft kiss. Was he that special someone?

'It's my worst regret.' He sighed and balled his hands into fists. 'I enlisted because I knew there wasn't a chance in hell he'd let me back into that house so I thought if I made enough money to buy her a house she could get out. Be free. Tend the garden any damn way she wanted to.'

Ah…the garden. That's where Plants to Paws came from. Her own eyes filled with tears as she thought of just how much it must've destroyed him to learn that the charity garden was going to be paved over to make way for a car park. And by whom. She made a silent vow to double the guest list. Come what may, they were going to save Plants to Paws and ensure it was there for the patients at the Clyde for ever.

'So did you get the house?' Esme asked quietly.

He shook his head. 'Cancer hit first and though I'd bought the house she was in a hospice and she passed away before I could even show it to her. At least I got to be with her then. My stepdad didn't handle the messy business of dying all that well so he wasn't around much.' A sad smile teased at his features. 'It was back to just the two of us in the end. She was so weak I bought her one of those miniature Japanese gardens. You know the little zen ones with stones and a bonsai tree and whatnot? She tended that thing as if her life depended on it.'

'Oh, Max.' There was nothing she could say to make any of it better. Her own experience with pain had taught her sometimes it was best not to say anything at all. Being there and listening was the best thing to do.

'After she died, I began to notice more and more patients wishing, above anything, that they could grow something. Keep something alive since they were powerless to do the same for themselves. So I sold the house to build Plants to Paws.'

No longer able to hold back, she wrapped her arms around him. 'I'm so sorry you've been through that. Let me assure you we will do everything in our power to make this the best Christmas ball ever. Gavin Henshall be damned!' She threw a fist in the air, hoping to tease out a bit of relief from the sadness he'd been carrying all of these years. There was a change. The tiniest flicker of something she couldn't put her finger on shifted through his eyes as he pulled her to him for a kiss.

Max had never once considered the possibility that feeling vulnerable could also make him feel strong. Opening up to Esme in the way he had had paid emotional dividends he'd never considered. There'd been a moment—right when he admitted he'd known who Gavin Henshall was all along—when he'd thought he'd lost her, but she'd silenced whatever was going on in that head of hers and heard him out. For that alone, Esme would always have a special place in his heart.

'C'mere.' Esme beckoned him over to the long wooden counter. 'What shoe size are you?'

'Eleven.' He couldn't help smiling at Esme's puckish face. After his big emotional purge she'd said she was more than happy to carry on talking but he'd had enough and suggested they do something she wanted to do. So here they were, preparing for an after-hours ice skate. He was bound to spend more time on his rear than his feet, but…what the hell. Her eyes had glittered with excitement at the idea so there was zero chance he was going to say no.

She handed him the skates then pulled a pair off of the shelf for herself. 'I can't believe we're doing this!' She clapped her hands and let out a quiet little 'Woohoo!' She'd promised the security guards they'd be as quiet as dormice. The fact she was Esme Ross-Wylde and had arrived carrying a big plate of Mrs Renwick's Christmas biscuits had had a lot more to do with receiving their go-ahead than keeping the volume down.

The pair of them went out to the moonlit skating rink…completely free and clear of any marks from the evening's crowds. Perfect for a bit of midnight mischief.

'I haven't done this for years!'

'Why has it been so long?'

Max recognised the shadows of sadness instantly.

'I used to come out here with my brothers.' She sighed and put a tidy bow on her second lace and clapped her hands to her knees. 'I haven't really told you about Nick, have I?'

'No. But if it's too difficult to talk about…'

'It is, but… I think the two of you would've got along. He was army. Like you. Worked in the canine bomb disposal unit.'

Max nodded. It was pretty easy to see where this was going.

'He was killed on Christmas Eve when I was eighteen and Charles was in the throes of med school.'

'That's rough.' And explained why she was so desperate for Christmas to be magical. She was trying to recapture a time that used to be. A memory of when life had been perfect. A bit like him, he supposed. Pretending Christmas wasn't happening never made the pain go away, so perhaps she had the right idea. Try and try again. One day it just might work.

'He was my hero. He was so much older than me, everything he did seemed amazing. When he died we all fell apart. Dad worked himself into an early grave. Charles buried himself in his medicine and I…'

Her voice caught as he saw tears form in her eyes. He put his arm around her and swept his hand along her cheek. 'It's completely understandable if you were sad, darlin'. Losing someone you love is pure heartache.'

Esme looked him straight in the eye. 'I was more than sad. I lost the plot.'

'I doubt that. Grief is a powerful emotion. Sometimes it is difficult to know how you're coming across to the world when everything seems so grey.' The only thing that had saved him after his mum had passed was Plants to Paws. Knowing he was putting some good back into the world after channelling so much hate in Gavin's direction.

Esme took one of his hands in hers and said, 'There's something I have to tell you.'

He nodded for her to go ahead. She'd been amazing when he'd bared some of his darkest memories to her and she deserved his full attention.

'I met a man shortly after Nick was killed. He said all the right things, did all of the right things. He made me feel safe. Cared for in a world I wasn't so sure about any more. If Nick, my amazing strong, incredible brother, could be killed, what else could happen?'

A surge of protectiveness shot through him. 'This man didn't hurt you, did he?'

She shook her head and covered her face with her hands. 'It's more embarrassing now than anything.'

'Hey.' He crooked a finger under her chin and ran his thumb along her cheek. 'Like I said, I like you just the way you are.'

She gave his arm a squeeze. 'I know. And that means a lot. In fact, it was your honesty with me that made me want to tell you my story. I owe it to you.'

Esme was trembling as Max took her hands in his and said, 'You don't owe me anything, love. Not one thing.'

'That's exactly why I *want* to tell you. Because you don't want anything from me. This man did.' Before she chickened out, she took in a deep breath and told him everything. 'I married him at the ripe age of nineteen. We eloped to Gretna Green, if you can believe it. Such a cliché!'

He gave a small shrug. 'You were young, and clichés are clichés for a reason. It was meant to be romantic, right? An act of love.'

Bless him. He was trying to find a silver

lining. Little did he know this particular cloud was completely shrouded in darkness.

'It was romantic,' she admitted miserably. 'And then pretty quickly it wasn't. Mostly because there wasn't love. Not that I knew that yet. At his suggestion, I quit veterinary school and we—meaning I—rented a ridiculous penthouse in Glasgow. When we went home and told everyone, my family were actually pretty amazing. We'd all been so sad after Nick's death it was great to have a reason to celebrate. And Harding took his time before his true colours were revealed.'

'Harding MacMillan? Isn't he the guy who's always on the covers of those socialite magazines?'

Esme looked at him in surprise. 'You read those?'

'You'd be surprised what pops up as reading material in the staffroom on a night shift.' He gave a self-deprecating laugh then admitted, 'It's not my usual fare, but I recognise the name.'

'If you'd been reading those same magazines eleven or twelve years ago you would've also recognised my name.'

He shook his head. 'They don't make much of a show in the Middle East conflict areas. Anyway, most of the stuff that's in those magazines is salacious gossip. Even if I had read it, I would've taken everything with a grain of salt.'

She fretted at the knitted cap resting in her lap. Being betrayed in the way she had had opened up all the wounds she'd thought were healing after Nick's death. Turned out…they hadn't even begun to heal. The entire experience with Harding had only served to magnify the pain she'd felt at the loss. 'Harding made me feel completely useless. And when, after it was all over, he sold his story to the tabloids with his own special spin, it made my life a living hell.'

Max stiffened. 'Why? What happened?'

'Not that he'd put it this way, but it turned out all of the wooing—fancy dinners, nights out on the town, weekends away—were all paid for with credit cards on the brink of being maxed out. He would fill one up then apply for another. Long story short, he married me because he wanted money. My family's money.'

A bitter laugh caught in her throat as she remembered the day she'd found out how his family came to be 'titled'. His father had bought the title years ago, along with one acre of woodland back when his business had been flourishing. He had since sold the same acre and title when the business had been failing. Not that Harding had bothered to tell anyone about the change of circumstances. If he hadn't been so deceitful about his family's lack of finances, she might've felt sorry for him, but Harding MacMillan had been one hundred per cent snake. A snake whose venom had no antidote.

She met Max's solid, kind gaze and shivered. Could this be the man she could finally put her trust in?

Max tucked a lock of her hair behind her ear then snuggled her hat back on her head. 'Wouldn't want you catching cold,' he explained, then continued after a moment's thought. 'You know it's not your fault, right? He was preying on a vulnerable young woman. I'm surprised he's not in jail.'

Her lips thinned. She would've pressed charges but…she'd given him her card. A joint account. It hadn't really been theft when it was a joint account. It would've boiled down to a case of him against her and Harding was very persuasive. It was how he'd convinced all the paparazzi to appear every time they'd gone to dinner or a club. She'd thought it was coincidence.

A sour taste filled her mouth as the worst of the memories returned.

'Because I wasn't at uni any more, I wanted to do something amazing for Nick. His service dog had meant the world to him and I'd heard about soldiers suffering from PTSD who needed their own service dogs so I decided to open a clinic to help them do that.'

'Which you did.'

She shook her head. 'No. Remember, this was years ago, in Glasgow. I became obsessed with the idea. I was working crazy hours with a local organisation to learn how to train the dogs so Harding "volunteered" to take over setting up the clinic. Leasing the facility, kitting it out. That sort of thing. I was so wrapped up in the dogs and trying to drum up publicity for the service sog centre that I didn't bother checking up on him.' She felt absolutely sick remembering it all. How the man could've done what he had, knowing it was in aid of her brother's memory.

'Did he get you a site?'

'Oh, he did that all right.'

'You don't sound like you were very happy with it.'

'I was at the time. It was all so romantic, and he had made such a show of wanting to take anything stressful out of my hands so that I could focus on the dogs and helping soldiers.'

Max nodded. He'd fallen for a lot of stuff, too. It had made him wary, but it had also taught him that anyone could fall for a con-man.

'He said he didn't want me to see it until the grand opening. That he wanted to see the surprise in my eyes. Oh, he saw surprise all right. So did all the society magazines.'

'I thought you said you'd invited the media.'

'I had. He'd found my list, cancelled them all and replaced them with his people. So, there I was, ready to cut the ribbon, glass of champagne in my hand, the whole nine yards… Harding had hung this huge, ridiculous red velvet curtain in front of the building and when he pulled it open...' her voice caught at the memory but she continued as if she had just swallowed sour milk '...instead of my humble canine therapy centre there was a gaudy, glitzy nightclub called Wylde.'

Max swore under his breath. That was a whole new breed of low.

'So, of course, once the legitimate papers got hold of the fact I'd opened a nightclub instead of the service dog centre, they dismissed me as just another airhead heiress who had more money than sense. It still makes me furious for not having seen through him before I put that stupid ring on my finger. Sure,' she acquiesced, 'it was a whirlwind romance. Maybe...three or four weeks? Insanity really, but I thought he loved me when all along it turned out it was my money he loved.'

Much to her embarrassment, tears began to trickle down her cheeks. And then flow. She hadn't cried about this in years but telling Max was strangely cathartic. Cleansing even. She'd felt so small back then. Humiliated and worthless. But she'd changed. She'd finally made something of her life. Which was a lot more than she could say for Harding. If her mother's short emails were any sort of guide, Harding was still living with little beyond his charm to keep him afloat. A hollow life if there was one.

Max pulled out a clean cloth handkerchief and handed it to her. Her heart squeezed tight. He was such a gentleman. Why couldn't she have fallen for someone like him back then? She thought back to the story he'd just told her and realised he probably wouldn't have been in a chivalrous place back then. Perhaps, despite the pain, they'd each needed to go through these tribulations to become the people they were now. A bit wiser. A bit more wary.

'I presume your family took him to task,' Max said after wiping away a couple of her stray tears.

She shook her head. 'I didn't want them to. It would've compounded the whole poor little rich girl thing having my family swoop in to rescue me. Particularly given the fact that, at the time, Mum was showing up at one too many nightclubs herself.'

'Did Harding actually think you would go for it? The nightclub, I mean?'

She shrugged. 'My best guess is that he thought I was so under his spell I would go for it to make him happy. He thought the service dogs thing was a fad.'

'Sounds like he didn't know you at all.'

She gave him a sad smile. 'We can definitely agree on that. The whole thing was so humiliating. Afterwards, once we'd split up and I'd come back here, it still took ages to shake everything off. The tabloids were paying people to get staff jobs here at Heatherglen. Undercover maids hoping to find me curled up in a weeping, sobbing ball in the corner of my gold-plated bedroom. That sort of thing. The last thing I wanted the world to see was me being pathetic, so I got myself back into veterinary school and set up the clinic properly. With no publicity.'

Max laughed and gave his head a rueful shake. 'That's my girl.'

Despite the seriousness of the talk, Esme blushed. His girl? She liked the sound of that. Even if it was just a saying, there was something safe and comforting about talking with

Max that she'd never felt with another man. It felt *real*. *Genuine*. As if there was nothing she could tell him that would make him think any less of her.

'I'm hoping he didn't get to any of your money in the end.'

'Oh, he did. Not all of it obviously,' she snorted and looked at the castle, glittering like a jewel in the crown. 'The joint account we shared was actually my trust fund. I never really spent much from it. Unlike Harding, I wasn't really one to splash the cash about.' She qualified the statement, so Max didn't get the wrong idea. 'I'm not unaware that I have grown up with a privileged lifestyle. I mean, how many people get an ice rink and an entire Christmas carnival outside their castle at Christmas?'

Max laughed appreciatively. There was warmth in it. As if he didn't care if she was worth a billion or tuppence. It was her he liked, not the trimmings she came with.

She shook her head. 'I still can't believe I fell for such a superficial poser.'

'Everyone has someone who pulls the wool over their eyes.' Max gave her back a soft rub and dropped a tender kiss on her forehead. 'He really put you through the mill, didn't he?'

'Yup!' She stood up, using one of Max's strong shoulders as support to keep her balance on her blades, and gave him a proper smile. 'But that was then and right now we've got a skating rink calling our names.'

They spent the next hour having an absolute ball, whirling and racing and falling down and kissing. It was every bit as fun as it had been when she'd sneaked out with her brothers to do exactly the same thing, minus the kissing part obviously.

That night when they made love it felt even more intimate than it had the night before. There was true sentiment behind the soft touches, the caresses, the deep, emotionally charged kisses they shared.

She was falling for him. Head over heels. The practical part of her knew she needed to put on the brakes and acknowledge that this was nothing more than a no-strings-attached fling. There was no way it could work in real life. His life was in Glasgow, hers was very much here at Heatherglen and, well, there was all the magic of Christmas that would melt away in the spring.

And yet…there was a tiny sliver of hope she hadn't felt in years. Hope that she might finally leave her scars from the past where they belonged. In the past. Hope that true love *was* real. That she deserved it. She stared at the lights twinkling on the tiny Christmas tree by the fireplace. Honestly? She wanted to believe in Christmas miracles. And Max was the man she wanted by her side when all of it came to pass.

CHAPTER NINE

'SOMEONE LOOKS HAPPY,' Charles growled as he dug his spoon into a rather enormous, well-sugared bowl of Mrs Renwick's delicious porridge.

'Someone else looks like they woke up on the wrong side of the bed.' Esme smiled benignly in return. She was in a gorgeous floaty love bubble. Four days in and her days with Max had morphed into a lovely little routine. Sometimes he spent time with her in the vet surgery and at others they worked on training with Euan and Fenella. Max usually had his meals with them, but he always, every single night, crawled under the covers with her. Not even a grumpy older brother whose mood had plummeted daily since he'd returned from his medical conference could burst the particularly lovely mood. 'Would you pass the blueberries, please?'

'They're out of season,' Charles snapped.

'So's your mood,' Esme chirped, tacking on a 'tra-la-la-la-la' to prove her point.

Charles grimaced, ate a spoonful of porridge, then pushed it away.

'What's up with you?'

'Nothing. Busy day, that's all.'

She was about to retort that all their days were busy but it didn't mean they had to be miserable but she opted for the kinder, gentler version of her kid sister self. She, after all, had three more glorious days of naughty nights and flirty days ahead. Charles, on the flip side, showed no signs of even as much as casting the slightest glance at a woman, let alone falling in love again. 'Anything I can do to help?'

'No. Thank you, though.' He pushed up and away from the kitchen table then turned back. 'I had a meeting with Fenella, by the way. I've put a call through to the Clydesbank to send up her records. She's agreed to let me take a second look at her meds.'

'Oh! Great.' Her gut instinct was to run out the door, find Max and tell him immediately, but the fact she and Max had agreed to keep their romance low key kept her in her chair, smiling dreamily up at her brother. 'You're the best.'

He narrowed his eyes. 'Are you sure you're all right?'

'Never better.' She took a huge spoonful of porridge so she couldn't answer any more questions. The truth of the matter was, no matter how much she told herself she shouldn't, she was falling in love.

Max was spending the day with Euan and Fenella as their training with the dogs intensified. He was being absolutely brilliant, ensuring they felt they were receiving proper support, asking questions for them when they were too shy to do so themselves. They were lucky to have a man like him in their corner. She was lucky to have a man like him in her bed! And utterly insane to let a man whose life was so solidly based elsewhere into her heart.

The morning at the veterinary clinic whooshed by and, as Aksel was now on hand to help, she was treating herself to an afternoon at the Christmas carnival where they were going to put Euan and Fenella's dogs through their paces.

She had just changed out of her scrubs into a cosy pair of leggings and a thigh-length jumper with a Christmas tree knitted into the pattern when she heard a knock on her office door.

'Come in.'

Her heart skipped a beat when she saw it was Max. 'Hello there, you. How's tricks?'

'You're looking festive as ever.'

She skipped over to him and gave him a quick peck on the lips. 'Mmm…chocolaty.'

'Margaret just made us all hot chocolate before "The Big Adventure".'

Esme pulled a sad face. 'I wanted to be the first one to make you hot chocolate! It's the one feather in my cooking cap.'

'Not to worry. I'm sure I'll be up for another before I head back south.'

Her sad face gained traction. 'I can't believe it's all coming to an end so soon.'

'I know.' Max pulled her into a cosy hug. 'It's not going to be nice, saying goodbye.'

She pulled back so she could look him in the eye and asked the one question she'd vowed to herself she wouldn't. 'Do we have to? Say goodbye?'

'I don't really see another way around it. Your life is here. My life's in Glasgow.'

'You don't fancy practising somewhere up here?'

The second the question was out she regretted it. It wasn't fair to ask him to change his life because of what they'd both known would, at best, be a festive fling.

He swept her hair off her forehead as his own brow crinkled. 'I think you know the answer to that, but let's talk about it tonight.' He tilted his head towards the door. 'We've got a very eager Fenella and Euan waiting out in Reception with their hounds, ready for the carnival.'

Though he sounded the same and looked the same, Esme's stomach twisted with anxiety. She'd overstepped the mark. Pushed when she should've accepted the situation for what it was. Doing her best to mask her misplaced disappointment that he hadn't immediately suggested that they scrap all their sensible, practical plans so they could get on with the business of falling in love, she said, 'Absolutely. Let's get on out there and enjoy some Christmas cheer, Heatherglen style!'

* * *

Max would've had to have been blind not to see the splinters of dismay pass through Esme's eyes when he put off answering her question. A dodge was a dodge and with her history, looking shifty was never a good thing. Of course he wanted to drop everything and stay in the magical world of Heatherglen—a place whose sole remit appeared to be making dreams come true. Whether it was to recover from PTSD, heal from a traumatic injury or meet that one faithful companion who would never lie, never cheat, never say one thing and mean another...

Damn. He was either going to have to grow a backbone and test the remaining elasticity in his heart or stick to his guns and go with their original plan: enjoy the here and now— then get back to real life.

Esme was bright enough as the group walked towards the Christmas carnival, each with a dog on a lead. Dougal, as ever, was lavishing love on whoever looked at him.

Esme threw Max the odd smile, but he couldn't see the light hitting her eyes like it normally did and it was killing him.

Of course he wanted whatever was blossoming between them to continue. More than anything he wanted to throw caution to the wind, pull her into his arms and tell her he loved her. Because he did. He knew it right down to the very last fibre in his body. He loved Esme Ross-Wylde heart and soul. So… what was the problem, then?

She'd been amazing when she'd heard his story. Didn't seem to give a monkey's that he'd come from a poor background. Or that he'd had a complicated, messy upbringing. Just as he loved her exactly the way she was, she seemed to care for him solely because of the man he was now.

So why was he holding back his feelings and, more importantly, his concerns when he knew honesty was the best policy with her? The only policy. The one way to know if Esme believed in him. Loved him even.

And then it hit him. Somewhere, deep inside him, he still hated Gavin Henshall for all he'd done to his mother. Worse than that, he was still beating himself up for not finding a way to forgive the man as his mother had asked him to. Forgive him and move on. It had been her last request and he'd failed her. Failed himself. And if it weren't for Esme's timely intervention, he'd very likely be failing everyone at Plants to Paws as well.

Esme had had an awful time with her brother's death and her subsequent marriage. She'd harnessed her anguish and turned it into something good. He'd thought he'd done the same with Plants to Paws, but without Esme? He'd be back at the Clyde clearing out the greenhouse and telling everyone the bad news. Again and again in his life, money and power had trumped good intentions. Could it be that love and its ally, forgiveness, were more important than both?

The thought hit him with the force of a lightning bolt. Was he strong enough to accept that having to start over didn't necessarily equate to failure? That the journey was every bit as important, if not more so, than the outcome? That he might be hurt by love again but that it was completely worth the risk?

Unless the answer was a solid yes, he wouldn't be able to love Esme the way she deserved to be loved. With all of his heart.

Because there'd always be a part of him wondering if he'd done enough to deserve her. Acknowledging that simple fact just about killed him. He watched as Esme led their motley crew towards a small log cabin where people could make gingerbread houses. After everyone entered, she looked back. 'Aren't you coming?'

He shook his head. 'I've got something to do. Can I meet you later?'

She gave a little nod, her features closing in on each other. Proof, if he'd needed it, that she knew something wasn't quite right.

'Are we okay?' she asked.

The anxiety in her voice near enough slashed his heart in two.

'We're okay,' he said, because he couldn't say what he wanted to. That he loved her. That he was going to have to find a way to reach down into his past and pull out some of his darkest memories, confront them, and pray that he came out stronger.

Esme poured a pile of cereal into her bowl then sloshed some milk in. It looked revolting. And it was her favourite cereal.

Something weird was up with Max. They'd spent the night together, but he'd not brought up whether or not he wanted to see her any more after Christmas. Something about the intensity in the way he'd looked at her, touched her, had made her feel as though he was memorising her in preparation to say goodbye.

All of which had her in a particularly foul mood.

She stared at the cereal then at Wylie. 'Want my cereal?'

He wagged his tail. She gave it to him.

She looked around the kitchen for something else to eat. Her eyes eventually landed on her gingerbread castle. Why make a house when you can build a castle? she'd thought. Fenella and Euan had thought it was hilarious. Max had given it a glance, her a smile and then told her he wouldn't be joining her in the veterinary clinic today as he'd volunteered to cover Lyle Sinclair's medic shift at the ice skating rink. Lyle wanted to tag along with Cass, who was due to rehearse for the Living Nativity down at the village. Fussing more like. Doting. Caring, adoring, lovesick man that he was.

She'd thought it was adorable about twenty-four hours earlier. Today? Not so much. She wrenched off the gingerbread turret and took a bite.

There was a light knock on the kitchen door. Max stuck his head into the room. 'I was just going to make a call to the Clyde then head out to the skating rink. Everything all right?'

'Not particularly,' she said, tacking on a petulant smile. He blinked his surprise.

Okay, fine. It wasn't a particularly mature way to respond, but she wanted Max to feel as bad as she did. She pulled a section of the wall off her gingerbread castle and chomped down on it.

Charles appeared behind Max, who let him through to the kitchen. 'Good to see healthy eating is still the order of the day,' he said in a remarkably similar strain of crankiness. 'May I?' He nodded at the castle.

She shrugged. 'Help yourself.'

He did, and the castle collapsed.

Her expression must've been one of pure

fury because both Charles and Max made their apologies and left. It wasn't the castle she was cross about. It was not having the guts to have it out with Max and find out what was going on with him. She'd thought they were good at being open with one another. Telling each other the truth. And here she was exactly where she didn't want to be. Feeling scared. Panicked she wasn't enough. Would never be enough for someone when all she wanted was to be enough for one man. For Max.

A horrible thought landed in her head. What if the only reason he was doing this was to make sure he got the money for Plants to Paws? Surely he knew her well enough to know she didn't offer lifelines like the Christmas ball with strings attached. The fact they seemed to adore each other's company was just an added bonus.

All of which meant she was being ridiculous. A bit of insecurity went a long way in her case, and it was time to keep it in check.

Doom and gloom would get her nowhere. It was probably nothing. Max was a busy man, who was doing his best to be as present as he could be here as well as keep tabs on his very busy life back in Glasgow. A life he'd dropped to give two of his patients this amazing opportunity.

See? Proof, if she'd needed any, that she was being ridiculous. He'd made just about the sweetest love to her a girl could imagine only a handful of hours ago. No one could be that intimate, that loving and also be looking for an escape plan.

Right! She took one last bite of her gingerbread castle, wiped her hands then announced to Wylie that it was time to go out and make the world a better place. No point in spreading her ridiculous mood any further than this kitchen. She knelt down so she was eye to eye with her big, furry bear of a dog. 'I'm being silly, aren't I, Wylie?' He rubbed his nose against hers. 'He's *not* Harding. All this silly insecurity is nothing, right?' He licked her chin. 'Well, that settles it. Just a blip on the old emotional barometer.' She called him to heel and together they walked to the veterinary clinic. When she passed Max, who was on his way to the ice-skating rink with the reflective safety vest on, she waved and smiled. She'd apologise for being such a grump later. In bed. He threw her a confused wave in return but seemed happy that her mood had improved.

'See, Wylie? Nothing to worry about. Absolutely nothing at all.'

With half an eye on the skating rink and half an eye on the veterinary clinic, Max's gut was churning with indecision. Should he tell her why he hadn't brought up their relationship last night or would it scare her off? Carrying around rage and fury over something he would never be able to change was not going to help anyone. Least of all him and Esme. He wanted to give this a shot. Be the man she deserved. Woo her properly. Take her out. Show her his favourite places in Glasgow. Discover her favourite walks up here. Hold hands at the movies. It'd be tough with his schedule at the Clyde but putting a few thousand commuter miles on his old four-by-four was worth it. Especially if he were to accept in advance that there was always the possibility it might not work out. Once the charity ball was over and he was back to work, they might discover their lives were simply too different for them to be a perfect match. It didn't mean their time together had been for nothing, but it did mean talking about the future at this juncture was a bit of a moot point. Live in a fairy-tale for ever? Sure. Why not? Commute two hours there and back every day to hold hands with his girl? Maybe yes. Maybe no.

He looked up as a few squeals erupted from the ice rink. A gaggle of girls had collapsed into a giggling heap of jewel-coloured winter jackets and scarves. They looked as though they didn't have a care in the world.

He wondered if Esme had ever had a chance to be that silly. The other night she'd told him that, as children, the local paper had always taken a picture of them going to church on a Sunday and had made note of the times they didn't. Never mind the fact they'd often been down in Glasgow, working for a soup kitchen. No wonder she cherished those stolen moments of fun on the ice rink with her brothers. No one to perform for.

For every ounce of him that had bones to pick with his own childhood, he wouldn't have traded it for hers. At least his most tumultuous years had only been under two people's radars. His mum's and his stepdad's. The press? It must've been awful. And incredibly impressive that she'd managed to turn it back round in her favour in the form of her annual Christmas ball.

It was tomorrow night. Maybe that's why she'd been so crisp this morning. It was a lot to organise. And the pressure had to be immense. They'd have to raise a lot of money if they wanted to put Gavin and his car park plans out of the picture.

He sensed someone approaching from behind him. 'Well, here she is.' He put his arm out and while Esme didn't snuggle close in to him her smile was sincere enough. She was all kitted out in her canine therapy centre winter gear and he was on duty so fair enough. She gave him a little hip bump. 'Sorry about earlier.'

He looked at her blankly. 'What do you mean?'

'Oh, don't be silly. You know I snapped at you.'

'I suspect your plate is rather full with the ball tomorrow.'

'It is,' she agreed, 'but that wasn't what I was grumpy about.'

'Want to talk about it?'

She scrunched up her nose. 'Not really. I was being silly. Imagining things.'

'About?'

'Absolutely nothing.' She gave his hand a squeeze. 'Just…sorry. I don't want there to be anything funny between us, seeing we haven't got much time left.' It was all he could do not to pull her into his arms and tell her he was confronting his very worst demon so that maybe they wouldn't have to call it a day. That Christmas, for once, would be the herald of good things to come for both of them.

He followed her eyes as they travelled out to the skating rink. She was watching a middle-aged couple skating along hand in hand. 'That's a first date.'

'How do you know?'

'He's showing off for her.' Her voice took on a dreamy quality. 'And the way she's looking at him…it's like she's won the lottery.'

Esme was right. The woman was beaming. More so when her beau pulled a bit ahead of her to do a bit of a jazzy move. Judging by his windmilling arms, it wasn't going to plan. The woman pulled ahead to do her own move. She put her arms out ballerina style, gave a couple of strong strokes of her skate blades and lifted her back leg into a lift when all of the sudden the giggling teens and happy couple collided and became a sprawled mass of bodies in the centre of the rink.

Max was on the ice with his medical bag in seconds. His rubber-soled boots didn't have brilliant traction, but they got him where he needed to be.

Max could hear Esme instructing the rink monitors to clear the other skaters from the ice.

The teens were examining themselves for injuries.

The gentleman was sandwiched between them all as he had tried to fling himself protectively over his girlfriend. When he rolled off, he howled in agony. 'My shoulder!'

Max shot a quick glance at his partner, who looked a bit dazed but was pushing herself up to a seated position. 'Can you let me have a look?'

The man stared at him blankly. 'Only if you can make it stop.'

Max made a quick examination. 'You've popped your shoulder out, mate. I don't think your wrist is looking all that brilliant either.'

'It's my shoulder that hurts most. Make it stop. Make. It. Stop.' The man's breathing was coming in short, sharp huffs as he tried to grapple with the pain. He launched himself forward so that his forehead and shoulder rested on the ice bearing some of his body weight.

'It's not the easiest way to treat you, pal. What do you say we try to—? Oops. Okay. Stay as you are if that helps you to breathe.'

Esme appeared beside him. 'I've called an ambulance from the hospital up the road. They'll try to get here in twenty minutes or so.'

'Brilliant. I should be able to get everyone

triaged before they come. Relocate this chap's shoulder, at the very least.'

'Anything I can do?'

Max did a quick scan of the group who were still sprawled on the ice. One teen was clutching her elbow. Another had her hand pressed to her forehead with a bit of blood appearing between her fingers. The woman who'd been trying to do a trick move was squeezing her knee into her chest. He tilted his head towards his medical bag. 'Do you mind popping on some gloves and pressing some gauze to that poor girl's forehead? I'll examine her in a second.'

'On it.'

Esme was swift and efficient. It was a shame vets weren't allowed to treat humans. Esme was every bit as confident with people as she was with animals. So much so he was happy to turn his full attention to the poor bloke and his shoulder, knowing she'd call him if something urgent was required.

'What's your name?'

'John.'

'All right, John. It looks like you've dislocated your shoulder and possibly fractured your wrist in your valiant attempt to be a bodyguard for your friend here.' Max shot a reassuring look in John's girlfriend's direction.

'That's my wife of over thirty years, I'll have you know!'

'Thirty years?' Max did a quick check on whether or not there was blood flow to John's arm. 'What's your secret?'

'Exactly that,' John huffed through his pain. 'Not having any secrets. Never once told her a lie. Jeanie's my absolute best friend. What she sees is what she gets. Isn't that right, darlin'? Oh— Ow!'

'That's right, lovebird. Nothing but honesty.' Jeanie gingerly pressed herself up to her hands and knees and began to crawl over.

'Hold steady there, John. Just checking for any other breaks or fractures. It looks like it's mostly your shoulder, although that wrist is beginning to swell.'

It was important he reduce the shoulder displacement quickly as that would no doubt swell as well. If that swelling were to cut off blood flow to the hand, it wouldn't be a very merry Christmas.

Jeanie crawled across to her husband. 'Are you all right, love?'

He tried to sit up and howled in pain.

'I'll take that as a no.' She shot Max an anxious look. 'It's our wedding anniversary. I was trying to show him how spry and delightful I was still was, even though I'm all wrinkly and grey-haired now.'

Max started talking John through the steps they'd need to take to alleviate the pain.

'You're as beautiful as you were the day I met you, darlin'.'

'If you can just hold still now, John, I'm going to check your vitals before I administer any pain medication.'

'Will it take long? We've got lunch reservations at the pub.'

Max smiled. 'I'm afraid you'd be best cancelling. I'll pop your shoulder back into place in the next couple of minutes, but you'll need X-rays to make sure there aren't any tears to the musculature and a stabilising sling at the very least.'

Esme was back at his side. 'What can I do?'

Max glanced at the ice rink as he slipped

on the blood-pressure cuff. No one else was there but John and Jeanie.

Esme explained, 'My elves helped me escort everyone off the ice. We've got them wrapped in blankets and waiting by the hot chocolate hut. I hope that's all right. I've also put a call in to Lyle. He's had similar medical training to you so can lend a hand if the ambulance gets caught up in traffic or anything.'

She was an amazing woman in a crisis. No surprise, given how incredibly calm and methodical she was in her own surgery.

'Doc! You're killing me.'

Max glanced down at the blood-pressure cuff that he'd been pumping up. 'Sorry, mate. Good news. Your readings are strong. We can administer some morphine sulphate to see if that helps ease the pain. We've also got some nitrous oxide in this kit here if I'm not mistaken. Just need a couple of more checks before we administer anything.'

'Please! Anything! No, Jeanie! Don't make me move.'

Jeanie had been trying to get him to sit up but the only way he could bear the pain was to put pressure on his shoulder. It looked like he was kowtowing to them all. John's peculiar position meant getting pain medication straight into the shoulder would be impossible. 'I'm going to have to inject into your gluteal muscles. Is that all right?'

'I don't care, just do it!'

'Oh, my poor big macho man. Leaping to my rescue like that.' Jeannie looked at Esme with tears in her eyes. 'Look what a hash I've made of showing off for him. Now his poor lily-white bum— Ooh, Doctor! Be quick about it or he'll get sunburn.'

'I'll be fast.' Exposing a man's derriere for any length of time on a sunny but very cold winter's day wasn't in anyone's best interest.

Esme was grinning. 'Is this your first date?'

'Oh, no,' said Jeannie as she stroked her husband's hair. 'He's been my man for over thirty years now. We had our very first date here, in fact. On this very day thirty-five years ago. That's why we picked this date for our wedding day.'

'I thought it was because you wanted a winter wedding,' John said, the painkiller clearly beginning to take effect.

Jeannie batted away the comment with a

smile. 'It's because of our happy memories here. Of course, it's a bit different now. Why, back in the day...'

Esme kept them talking while Max got himself into position to do the shoulder reduction. 'It all sounds very romantic.'

Max laid out a thick wool blanket on the ice. 'Right, John, I'm just going to roll you over onto your back here.'

After another round of agonised *No* and *Please Stop* and a couple of things not suitable for children, they got him there. Max slipped the face mask onto John that would allow him to breathe in some nitrous oxide. 'When you want to take a breath with the nitrous oxide, you press this button here. A few deep breaths and it should help your nervous system relax a bit.'

'What if it doesn't?'

Max shot a quick glance at Esme, who was waiting to hand him equipment from his medical kit. 'There's stronger stuff, but if we can avoid it, it'd be best.'

'You can do it, John,' his wife encouraged him. 'You'll not want to be on the strong stuff as we've got dinner with the Carmichaels on

Christmas Eve, then there's the Boxing Day lunch with the bridge club. Don't forget we're hosting the Hogmanay drinks do—'

John turned to Max, 'We might need that extra bit of painkiller if she carries on reminding me of all our social engagements!'

'John, you rascal. You know you love them. Just as much as you love me.' She planted a kiss on his cheek as if it settled the matter. Which, apparently, it did as John was visibly more relaxed. 'Right, then.' Max rubbed his hands together. 'Let's get this shoulder back where it belongs.'

After manipulating the arm to a ninety-degree angle then gently levering his forearm to the side, he felt the shoulder shift back into place.

'There you are.'

'That was it?' John looked at his arm, clearly expecting more.

''Fraid so, pal. There are more dramatic ways, but this one hurts the least.'

'Sounds like the voice of experience.'

'Army rugby.'

John nodded as if that explained everything. 'Our lads play rugby. They've dislocated just about everything that moves!'

'Well, don't try too hard to catch up with them. From the sound of things, you've got a busy Christmas schedule. Want to stay fighting fit for the wife, don't you?'

The silver-haired gent laughed. 'That I do, son. Thank you. You've rescued me from a world of pain.' After putting his arm in a sling and some ice on his wrist, John allowed himself to be gently helped up and escorted off the ice.

After the ambulance had come, and they'd gone through everything with Lyle Sinclair for the record, the rink opened again. Esme crooked her hand into Max's elbow and grinned up at him. 'Fancy a spin?'

'Maybe not today.'

'Good answer,' she said. 'I was thinking we could head into town and see the Living Nativity. Cass is in it and a couple of the lads from the vet clinic.'

'I'm not really sure the nativity is my thing.' He backpedalled when her smile dropped. *This may not last for ever, but you have it in your power to be kind.* 'But if you think it'll be fun, count me in.'

Esme could hardly believe how transformed Cluchlochry looked. It was straight out of a fairy-tale. Glittering lights everywhere. Tasteful decor binding the different shopfronts and buildings together in a harmonious seasonal aesthetic. She didn't think she'd ever seen so many holly and evergreen swags looping from window ledge to window ledge. It was gorgeous.

'So where's this nativity?'

'Just across there on the market square. Oh!' Esme clapped her hands. 'Look! Cass is Mary! She told me she was going to be the donkey.'

'I would've thought you'd have volunteered Wylie to be the donkey.' Max gave Esme's faithful canine companion a scrub on the head.

Esme smiled as Max moved Dougal's lead from one hand to the other so he could hold Esme's hand. He led them all across the square and found a place near the front where they could see the full tableau.

The Living Nativity was just that…a life-sized version of a nativity scene, with local villagers and their livestock standing in for the miniature versions of Jesus, Mary, Joseph, the three kings and, from the look of things, a candlestick maker—a woman Esme recognised from one of the shops who sold all sorts of products to do with bees.

Cass was glowing as Mary. As promised, Lyle had fashioned an old ladder, which wouldn't have looked out of place in a stable, into a perch for Cass so her leg wouldn't hurt. The tableau was only for an hour but even so…as she was still recovering from her injuries sustained during a search and rescue mission at the site of a massive explosion, there was no point in taking risks. Cass was so fiercely independent it was wonderful to see her allowing someone to help. Across the crowd from them Esme could see Flora and Aksel gently steering his daughter and her service dog to the front of the display so Mette could enjoy the new 'cast'.

The whole scenario made Esme feel peaceful. Content in a way she'd never felt before.

Just a girl out with her man, looking at the Christmas delights.

See? She *had* been ridiculous this morning, thinking Max was hiding something from her. Here they were, out in public, and he was more than happy to hold her hand as if they'd been a couple for ever. A warm, swirly, happy heat whirled though her when he popped a scratchy kiss onto her head. It was time to trust again. *Time to love.* She could hardly believe she was thinking it, let alone believing it.

She was in love with Max. Whether or not they could make anything of their relationship remained to be seen, but if this season was about anything it was about having faith. Faith and hope. Believing in the impossible.

'It's amazing, isn't it?' Esme looked up at Max.

'Absolutely. I've never seen anything like it. Do you see, they've even got a few wee early lambs over there?' Max pointed out the furry little beasts whose tails wriggled with delight when their mother was led into the small pen. 'They've done a brilliant job.'

'Apparently they need someone to stand

in for one of the three kings on Christmas Eve. I'm already signed up to be Mary.' Esme looked up at Max. 'Do you fancy coming back up here after the ball?'

It was a loaded question and, from the look on his face, one Max clearly hadn't expected. She'd actually wanted to ask him up for the whole of Christmas but was so used to being cautious the Christmas Eve invitation was about as brave as she could get.

'I'll have to check in with the hospital. See what sort of rosters they've put me on.'

'Of course,' Esme said brightly, quickly turning back towards the nativity. She didn't want Max to see the disappointment in her eyes.

'I did tell Andy I'd like to have a chat with him before I headed back to Glasgow.'

'You mean Euan's new bestie? Those two seem inseparable.'

'I know, a pair of odd bods, aren't they?'

She almost said you could say the same about the pair of them, but Max started rattling off a list of things he needed to do tonight before he packed up and headed back to Glasgow to dust off his kilt. Not quite the romantic gesture she'd been hoping for, but she'd been the one who'd insisted they bring Wylie and Dougal along to the Live Nativity, even though he'd suggested they leave them behind, so perhaps this was what real relationships were all about. Give and take. Compromise. Balance.

She twisted round so she was facing Max and gave his scarf a little tug. 'Sounds good. Shall we head back see if we can rustle up some you and me time tonight?'

He gave her a decidedly wolfish wink. 'Absolutely, my dear. Time's awasting.'

CHAPTER TEN

MARGARET PULLED THE strings tight and tied off the corset. She looked over Esme's shoulder into the full-length mirror and beamed. 'Oh, Esme. You look absolutely *amazing*. You're so lucky your family tartan brings out your blue eyes. Mine makes me look all pale and revolting.'

Esme laughed. 'It does not. You look beautiful. Green tartan and dark hair? A perfect combination. Besides—' she pointed out the obvious '—you're only wearing the sash and your parents won't be there. You could take it off if you want to. I won't tell if you won't.'

Margaret grinned. 'I just might do that.' Margaret picked up a bit of gingerbread from the remains of Esme's gingerbread castle then sighed as she looked back at Esme. 'You look like a blinking princess. Perfect, seeing as you're about to be in the arms of your Prince Alarmingly Charming.'

'Don't be ridiculous.' Esme swatted at the air between them then gave another little twist in front of the mirror. As silly as it was, for the first time in years she actually cared whether she looked beautiful or not. The setting for the ball had been specifically chosen to match the charity—the Kibble Palace at the Glasgow Botanical Gardens. She knew Max's mum had loved it there and had thought it would be the perfect place to tell Max she loved him. A spray of nervous energy gripped her chest as she silently walked herself through the plan. Host the ball. Give Max his cheque. Then, once all of the madness of the ball was over and done with, she'd say those three perfect words: *I love you.*

Plants to Paws would be saved, so he wouldn't 'need' her any more. His reaction would tell her in an instant whether or not he felt the same way about her as she did about him.

Tendrils of insecurity began to seep into place despite her very best tentions. Despite spending the night together, Max still hadn't brought up whether or not he thought the idea of seeing each other after he headed back to

Glasgow was a good idea. He didn't strike her as the type of man who would ghost a girl, but... No.

She stared at her reflection and gave herself a stern frown. Max Kirkpatrick was a gentleman. It could be that he didn't want to see her any more, but there was no chance he'd just up and leave her. A man who kissed a woman the way he'd kissed her when he'd left Heatherglen that morning was a man who would be coming back for more.

Margaret barked a loud and very unladylike laugh. 'What are you grinning at?'

'What? I'm not grinning.' She was. She was definitely grinning.

'You look like the cat who got the cream. Mind you, I'm perfectly happy, but with a man like Max about to appear in a kilt? I'd be grinning like the Cheshire cat as well.'

Esme tried to wipe the smile from her face but couldn't. 'He is rather scrummy, isn't he?'

There was a familiar knock on her bedroom door and, as usual, Charles didn't bother waiting for a reply before sticking his head in.

'We could've been naked!' Esme chided.

'Hmm. Well, you aren't.' Charles was clearly

distracted. So much so she wondered if he would have even noticed if they'd been naked. 'You lot ready to head down to Glasgow?'

'Come on. Let's see you in all your finery.' Margaret beckoned Charles in. He gave a half-hearted turn in his dress kilt then jangled the keys. 'All right, ladies? Your carriage awaits.'

'Is it a pumpkin now or is that at the other end of the evening?' Margaret loved winding Charles up. It used to be because of a lifetime crush on him. Now it was just for fun. Being loved up with the local GP did that to a girl. Made her permanently happy. Esme was pretty sure being in love with a Glaswegian A and E doc did exactly the same thing to her.

They both grinned at him.

Charles rolled his eyes.

Poor Charles. Esme hoped he found someone to love, too. Even though hers was still in the baby-steps stage, meeting and falling in love with Max had already filled her with brand-new confidence. It wasn't a pushy, braggart's confidence. It was more...peaceful. Settled. As if love had finally made her whole.

'Where's Max?' Charles scanned the room. 'I thought he'd be coming with us.'

Esme put on her best casual voice. 'He left late this morning. He said he had a couple of meetings in Glasgow so he drove Euan and Fenella back down. I'm sure he'll be there early. He said there was something he wanted to talk to me about, so...'

Charles shot her one of his intense, protective, big brother looks. 'What kind of talk?'

Again...that clammy feeling she couldn't quite shake pushed to the fore. 'It's probably nothing.'

'Like a sparkly diamond engagement ring kind of nothing?' Margaret cackled, and wriggled her fingers dramatically.

'Don't be daft!' Esme shot Margaret a thanks-for-nothing glare. 'He was here for Plants to Paws.'

'Yeah, right. You keep telling yourself that,' Margaret said dryly as she pulled her pashmina from the sofa and wrapped it round her shoulders. 'What do you think of Max, Charles?'

'Why?' Charles's big brother mode flicked onto high alert. 'What's he done?'

Esme glared at Margaret. She hadn't yet spelled things out to Charles. He was so protective. He still saw her as that messed-up nineteen-year-old, so she had wanted to be crystal clear what was happening with Max before she'd said anything.

She gave Charles an innocent smile. 'Nothing beyond looking forward to presenting him with a big fat cheque for his charity tonight.'

'I'll bet you're hoping to present a lot more than that,' whispered Margaret.

Despite herself, Esme giggled. Charles barely noticed, thank goodness. Margaret started humming 'The twelve days of Christmas', which made her giggle even more. That's more like it, Esme thought. Giggly, girly fun in advance of a beautiful Christmas ball. A big brother who was focusing on the right things. Fingers crossed, tonight would be the perfect evening before what could be the perfect Christmas.

'Forgive him.'

Max heard his mother's voice as clearly as if she were sitting right there on the bench beside him. In his mind's eye he looked up towards the hospice room where she had spent her last days then readjusted the lavish Christmas wreath with a rueful smile. What a difference a week made. Never mind the castle, the top-rate medical and canine facilities and the Christmas carnival. The only thing—the only *one*—he was impressed with had blue eyes, blonde hair and had pushed at the elasticity of his heart and mind so hard and fast he had no choice but to decide if he was up to changing.

'I know you find it hard to believe, but he loved me in his own way.'

Max's heart rate accelerated as an image of his stepfather closing the door on him when he'd returned from his first tour of duty popped into his mind.

'Always remember that the love we share is so much bigger than anything else. It has the power to heal. To lift. To inspire.'

His mother's words had been the inspiration behind Plants to Paws. If all went well tonight, the place could virtually run itself from now on so he'd need something new to work on. And for the first time in a long time he looked deep inside himself to get answers.

He needed to forgive Gavin. *Wanted* to forgive him. Unless he let go of all that rage, he was not fit to love. Not properly. He closed his eyes tight and pictured the complexity of feelings he had about Gavin as a grenade. The hurt, the anger, the fear. For well over half his life he'd let Gavin define whether he was a success or a failure. And in Gavin's world success meant money. Power. Failure meant living in a run-down inner-city estate where, no matter how hard you worked or how kind you'd been, you were at the mercy of developers who thought nothing of paving over another man's hopes and dreams.

His mental grenade went incandescent with pent-up fury.

Then he mentally pulled the pin.

Two seconds later?

The sun came out from behind a cloud.

Yes, he was still Max Kirkpatrick. Still an A and E doctor in an inner-city hospital. A soldier who'd served his country. A doctor who'd saved many lives. He was also a man who was in love with a woman who deserved his whole heart. Would letting go of his past be as easy as willing it to be over? He sure as hell hoped so. It was time to get on with his life. Live the future he'd always dreamed of. A future he hoped with every fibre in his being included Esme.

An entire glitter bomb exploded in Esme's bloodstream when she finally saw Max enter the ballroom.

The man most definitely knew how to wear a kilt. Yum.

As she worked her way through the crowd, thick with Scotland's most generous donors, she was vividly aware that the only person who really mattered to her tonight was Max.

'Hey, you.' She touched his arm.

When he turned and saw her, that heated buzz of electricity she now knew she didn't want to live without swept through her. It was time to change her life. Stop hiding out at Heatherglen and finally open the clinic in Glasgow she'd always dreamed of. Margaret and Aksel could run the Heatherglen site. She and Max could forge a life here. It'd be perfect.

Max leant in and kissed her cheek, the moment briefly closing out the rest of the world as she inhaled the scent that was so specific to him. The outdoors. A hit of citrus. Male inner strength.

With his cheek brushing against hers, he whispered, 'You look beautiful.'

She stepped back and gave a shy little twist in her dress. A nod to her family's tartan, the double skirts were in two shades of blue, the darker of the two rucked up so that the thick satin cornflower blue underskirt was visible as well. The under-bust corset was surprisingly comfortable now that she was used to it. It had been woven by a local woollen mill and showed off the family tartan to full effect. The appreciative look in Max's eyes meant wrestling into the ensemble had been worth the effort.

'Gorgeous, darlin'.' He dropped her a wink. 'Any chance you'll save a place for me on your dance card?'

They were hardly the words of a man who was about to tell her to take a hike so she crossed her fingers that he had decided they should see each other once the ball was over.

Besides, it was Christmas. He couldn't possibly break her heart at Christmas, could he? She gave him a coquettish smile. 'If you're lucky, I might even save you two.'

Charles came up to them and said something about wanting to introduce Max to someone. She watched as they worked their way through the crowd, wondering… hoping… Charles would see everything in Max she saw. A passionate man committed to making the world a better place despite the way life had kept knocking him down. No matter how many times it had happened, he'd still got back up again.

There was a part of her that was still shy of marriage, but her heart was speaking loud and clear. A life with Max Kirkpatrick would make her a better person. A happier person. Living with fear, not trusting anyone to come too close, never feeling worthy enough to deserve being loved for herself and herself alone…it had depleted her.

With Max she felt like a newborn colt. Better even. Giddy, full of verve and willing to take on a thousand new challenges she would have never considered before she'd met him.

A life that, perhaps, stretched beyond the gates of Heatherglen. Perhaps they should start tonight. Maybe, after they'd talked, she'd suggest they spend the night in Glasgow… give her a taste of all that lay ahead of them.

Max nodded and listened as Charles spoke.

'Do you understand what I'm trying to say?'

'Loud and clear.' There had been no malice in Charles's words. One could argue it wasn't even personal. He'd explained how far Esme had come. How this was a vulnerable time of year for her. That she was more trusting than she should be. Though Charles hadn't spelled it out, Max understood what Esme's very protective older brother was saying with laser-sharp clarity.

Hurt my sister and you'll have me to answer to. Your best bet is to back off. Now.

Hurting Esme was the last thing on his mind. Being pulled to one side as he had been—being pointedly reminded he was here to receive charitable aid for Plants to Paws and nothing more—was like a sharp knife finding that sweet spot between his ribs. Or, more pointedly, a wrecking ball to his plan to finally open his heart to Esme and say yes, to everything. Yes to dating. Yes to love. Yes to trying to build a future together. He knew it wouldn't be perfect. Not right away anyway. He lived here, she lived at Heatherglen. Neither of them could just drop their lives. But he had shored up enough strength over the past week to admit to her he was flawed, and she hadn't slammed the door in his face. Quite the opposite, in fact.

He looked across to where Esme was talking with Charles and a group of donors. She really was a remarkable woman. She had made all this happen. And she did it every year. Every day if you counted the animal's lives she saved, the humans she empowered with service dogs. How a woman like her could've thought for a second she wasn't worthy of love...

Now was the time to make the call. Was he in or was he out?

He soaked in the beautiful surroundings, the waiters floating about the place with trays of luxurious canapés and delicate crystal flutes of champagne. Charles hadn't said as much—and certainly didn't strike him as the type to judge—but this wasn't Max's world. These were Scotland's movers and shakers. The power people. He was a grassroots man. A guy who rolled up his shirtsleeves, grabbed a shovel and got stuck in. He gave a mirthless laugh. He was the guy who picked up the poop. Esme deserved someone who wanted more. Pushed harder. Thought bigger.

He was happy where he was. Serving Glasgow's not so finest. It was where he belonged. All of that boiled down to one thing. He would never be the man Esme deserved.

For the next hour or so, no matter how hard Esme tried to make good on that promise to dance with Max, she simply couldn't get anywhere near him. Again and again their eyes caught, but donors were virtually queuing up to talk to him about Plants to Paws. Those who couldn't get to him made a beeline for her. Told her what an inspired idea it was. Wondered if there were ways they could make similar gardens and pet visiting areas outside other hospitals. It made her feel so proud. All the charities she had championed were incredible, but this one had a special place in her heart. Before she'd as much as taken a sip of her champagne they'd surpassed their target. If things continued along these lines, Max would be able to set up ten Plants to Paws. It was truly inspiring.

Once again she sought him out in the crowd. She hoped this would be the proof he needed to finally realise just how valuable, strong and incredible a man he was. She hadn't been blind to his insecurities. To the little boy in him still trying to prove he was worth 'investing in'. He didn't only deserve all the money that was pouring in, he deserved every ounce of love she had for him. He probably didn't even know how much he'd helped her. Being here, feeling so confident in front of the media and the donors, she realised Max had helped her reach a place where she was finally able to see Harding MacMillan for what he truly was: a small, conniving, opportunistic man. If he hadn't pulled the wool over her eyes he would've pulled them over someone else's. His actions were a reflection of who he was…not her. And that simple revelation made all the difference.

All too soon it was time for speeches. Esme managed to pull Max away from a group of well-wishers and asked if he was ready to head up to the podium.

'Absolutely, I just…'

There was something off. Something he wasn't telling her.

'Max? Is everything all right?'

'I need to tell you something.'

'Miss Ross-Wylde?' The maître d' touched Esme's elbow and pointed towards the stage. 'Everyone's glasses are being charged for the toasts.'

'Of course.' She turned back to Max, whose expression had shifted from agitated to resolute. As if he'd made a decision and wasn't going to change his mind. 'Do you mind if we talk after the speeches?'

Before he could answer she was being ushered up onto the podium.

Esme's speech of thanks to the donors was short but entirely heartfelt. '…in closing, without you this inner-city haven would have been paved over. A car park or a garden? You have spoken loud and clear. Thanks to your generosity, every single one of the Clyde's patients will now have a permanent lifeline to a beautiful garden where they can grow vegetables or flowers, play with their pets, or simply sit and watch the world go by as they go through their journey in hospital.' As the audience applauded, she beckoned Max to step up to the podium. Plants to Paws existed because of him. He should be the one in the spotlight.

After making a few heartfelt comments of thanks, Max turned to Esme and raised his glass of champagne. 'My biggest thanks, of course, go to this beautiful woman right here. Without her...' His Adam's apple dipped and lifted as he swallowed and started again. 'Without her, a young lad's dream to put some good into the world would not have come true. In our time together she has shown me just how strong she is. Which is why I know she will continue to be a beacon of inspiration for all the people she will meet now that our time together has come to an end.'

Esme felt as though she'd been hit by a truck. What was he talking about?

He continued, 'I would like to propose a toast to a woman who I hope continues her incredible work. I know she will continue to bring change to people's lives. And I would like her to know that I will always remember her and the kindness she has shown Plants to Paws. The patients—'

A loud buzzing started in Esme's ears. *Always remember her?* Was this it? The last night she'd ever see him? She forced herself to tune back in again.

'…with her busy schedule I suspect our paths won't cross again, but she can rest assured that she will always be remembered.'

Esme grabbed hold of the podium, the floor no longer feeling stable beneath her feet.

Max was breaking up with her. And though no one here knew it, except perhaps Margaret whose eyes were all but popping out of her head, he was humiliating her in public. Just as Harding had done.

'Ladies and gentlemen, if could you all please charge your glasses and join me in a toast to Esme Ross-Wylde…'

He lifted his glass, took a sip without losing eye contact, then leant in to whisper, 'I'm so sorry.' Without waiting for a reply, he gave the crowd a quick wave then left the room.

It didn't make sense. None of it did.

Esme felt as though ice had filled her body. Once more she'd been played. Once more she'd misread a man from the moment she'd met him. Once again her heart was breaking. Only this time she knew she wouldn't be able to put it back together again.

Suddenly, urgently, all she wanted was to be back in her safe haven. Back at Heatherglen with her dogs and her big brother, where she was safe. If she never saw Max Kirkpatrick again it would be too soon.

CHAPTER ELEVEN

EVEN UNDER HEAVY attack from enemy fire, Max's heart had never beat faster. He was leaving the woman who was more than likely the love of his life.

Though his flat was miles away, he walked through the Botanical Gardens and back to his neighbourhood to see if it would give him any perspective. A few freezing hours later he was none the wiser.

Defeat weighted his every footstep and when he finally got home, he fell into a restless sleep.

He woke up feeling exhausted and empty. He forced himself out of bed, into the shower then out the door to Plants to Paws. It was where this whole debacle had begun. It was where he'd lay it to rest with a few hours' hard labour.

When he eventually returned home, covered in earth from a few hours of digging and planting some fruit trees one of the patients had brought in, he glanced at the racks of newspapers outside a shop near his flat. There she was, right on the front page. The photographer had captured her perfectly. Beautiful. Capable. Strong.

And he'd just hurt her in the worst way imaginable. In a situation where she couldn't do anything other than paste on a smile and bury her pain.

The self-loathing he felt at that moment was powerful enough to consume him but something rose in him that said, no. Enough. Esme deserved more and he was the man to give her what she wanted. Love. Pure, unconditional, everlasting love.

He raced back through the conversation he'd had with Charles. Had Esme's brother ever told him to back off? No. Had he said he thought Max wasn't a worthy suitor? Quite the opposite. He'd said he respected him. Admired what he did.

Then how the hell had he heard what he had? That he wasn't worthy?

Because it was his biggest fear.

Well, he didn't want to let fear run his life

any more. It had for far too long and today it was going to end.

If Esme decided she didn't want him in her life any more after what he'd done he'd have to take it. But he wasn't going to just let her walk away without letting her know how he really felt.

He dug into his pocket for his car keys and a short while later hit the motorway for Heatherglen.

He loved Esme. More powerfully than he had loved any woman. If his life had taught him anything it was that standing by and doing nothing was the worst course of action. With grim determination he punched an address into his sat-nav and set off on the make-or-break journey.

Esme drew up a dose of anaesthetic and was just about to put it into the IV bag already hooked up to Boopsy the Labrador when Aksel put his hand on her arm to stop her.

Esme stared at the syringe then looked at Aksel. She could only see his eyes thanks to his surgical mask and cap, but he looked alarmed.

'What?' They urgently needed to put the young Lab under after an X-ray had revealed his lethargy and lack of appetite were due to a tennis ball being lodged at the top of his intestines. Proof, if she'd needed any, that having fun came with consequences.

'You've prepared the wrong dosage.'

'No, I haven't.'

The vet nurse who was with them winced, then showed Esme the dog's chart. 'He's only twenty kilos, not forty.'

Esme dropped the syringe as if it were on fire.

She'd let herself get so distracted by her emotions she had compromised the poor dog's life.

The roiling ball of fury she'd been wrestling with ever since the ball last night had nearly overshadowed her number one vow: to care for and protect the animals she treated with every ounce of her being.

The nurse picked up the syringe, disposed of the contaminated needle and waited for instructions.

The last thing she wanted to do was harm someone's beloved pet. It was the final surgery of the day. She'd managed to hold things together so far, but endangering a poor, innocent creature because she couldn't focus? Unacceptable. She looked Aksel square in the eye and did something she'd never done before. 'Can you do the surgery? I think I need to sit this one out.'

He agreed and mercifully didn't go through any ridiculous show of hugging her or asking if she was okay or if she wanted to talk about it. She never, ever wanted to talk about this again.

She tugged on her thickest parka as the snow was falling *yet again*. Normally she'd be thrilled. Snow on Christmas Eve! Today it was just *irritating*. She glanced across at the Christmas carnival. It was all laughter and lights and couples holding hands and looking adoringly into one another's eyes.

She needed a walk with a dog. It was the only medicine that would get her to see straight. Especially as she had the Living Nativity to do tonight. Charles had said he'd ring to cancel for her, but she didn't want her big brother stepping in to fix things for her. She was a grown woman. A grown woman who should be able to deal with the fact she'd let a lying bastard into her heart yet again. From here on out? Total. Nun.

A few metres out from the clinic, Margaret ran out to meet her. 'You taking Wylie for a walk?'

That had been the plan but if she admitted that, Margaret would want to come along and that would involve talking.

Wylie took hold of the lead dangling from Esme's hand and tugged it. Margaret knew that meant it was walkies time.

'I'm coming whether or not you want me to,' Margaret said.

Esme huffed out a sigh.

Margaret gave her scarf another whirl round her neck and met Esme's speedy pace. 'Just so you know, I'm as cross as you are.'

Esme wheeled on her. 'Cross? You think I'm *cross* with him?' Her fist slammed against her chest. 'I trusted him. I opened up my heart to him. I *loved* him.'

'Charles? Of course you love Charles.'

Esme stopped cold. 'What are you talking about?'

Margaret returned her perplexed expression with an equally confused look. 'What are *you* talking about?'

'I'm talking about Max leaving the ball without as much as a thank you very much.'

Margaret shot a nervous look at the castle. 'Did Charles happen to tell you about the little talk he had with Max before the speeches?'

'No.'

Margaret's features morphed into a full-on wince. 'I thought you knew. That's why I didn't say anything.'

'About what?'

Margaret scrunched her forehead, clearly debating whose loyalty to play to.

'Margaret! What did Charles do?

An hour later Charles zipped Esme's fleece up to her throat as if she were a five-year-old. She batted his hands away. If she didn't love him so much she would give him a punch in the nose. If she were that sort of woman. Which she most definitely was not.

He pulled the zip up anyway. 'You're sure you want to do this?'

'Of course.' She tugged herself free and pulled on the burlap dress the Marys had been wearing. 'I promised the nativity committee I would do it. Unlike *some of us*, I do not let people down by telling them one thing then doing another!'

'I didn't realise you liked him in that way!'

'Even a blind person could see I loved him! Surely you were aware of it enough to give him that big brother talk of yours.'

'Wait. You love him?' Charles looked dumbfounded.

'Yes,' She'd never felt more certain of anything in her life. 'I love him, and I want to date him and go on holidays with him and wear silly Christmas jumpers with him. For many years to come, if possible.'

A clock chimed on the mantelpiece.

'Are you sure you want to be in the nativity? You're a bit high-strung. Do you think you'll be able to sit still?'

Esme glared at her brother. *Honestly.* 'If Mary could ride a donkey to Bethlehem when she was nine months pregnant, I can do an hour in the market square. And then I'm going to get in the car and drive to Glasgow and tell Max I love him.'

'You should ring him. It's snowing. The four-by-four hasn't been serviced in—'

'Uh-uh!' She cut him off. 'This is something that has to be done face to face. A phone call isn't good enough. Besides, you're the reason I'm in this stupid mess.'

'I didn't say anything!' Charles threw up his hands.

'According to Margaret, you told Max I was a fragile little piece of china that deserved the very best life had to offer!'

'Isn't that what a big brother is supposed to say to potential suitors?' Charles looked so bewildered it almost endearing. Almost.

'Don't you get it?'

'Obviously not.' He threw up his hands and plopped down on the couch.

'You scared him off! If you tell someone like Max—a man who's been trying to do right by the people he loves—that he isn't good enough—'

'I never told him he wasn't good enough, I just said…' The penny dropped. He scrubbed his face with his hands. 'I think I owe Max an apology.'

'Good! Then you can come along to Glasgow

and dig me out of any ditches if we hit any black ice.' Before Charles could protest, she pinned on a bright smile. 'Right! Let's get this show on the road.'

The crowd round the nativity was especially big. The magic of Christmas Eve had wrapped everyone in its embrace. As it was snowing, it had been decided that rather than take up one of the villagers' very generous offers to let her toddler be the baby Jesus, Dougal was standing in instead as he had a built-in fur coat.

Wylie had on a pair of antlers and was lying with his head in Esme's lap as she knelt by the manger. Charles was one of the three kings. She eventually had to stop looking at him as his eyes were laced with such concern it was about to do her head in. Breaking down in front of the whole of Cluchlochry wasn't part of the plan.

About twenty minutes in, the crowd started murmuring and parting as if they were letting someone through. Her eyes widened as Mrs McCann's shire horse appeared. It was dressed up like a camel one of the three kings might've arrived on. Only…all the kings were there. Charles, Hamish from the clinic and Lyle. Wylie lifted his head and gave a friendly woof. Dougal jumped up in the manger and began wriggling in that happy way he had when he saw someone he knew.

When she looked up and saw who this unexpected arrival was, her heart leapt straight into her throat.

Max.

Her gorgeous, manly, wonderful Max. He was wearing his kilt, which had to be ruddy cold as it was beginning to snow. Big fat flakes fell on her face as she fruitlessly tried to blink away her tears.

He got off the horse and handed the reins to Mrs McCann, who gave him an utterly adoring smile.

What on earth was happening? The last place she'd thought he would've wanted to be was with her.

Wylie, sensing she'd been thrown completely off-kilter, pressed his big furry nose against her thigh.

'I think I owe you an apology,' Max said when their eyes met.

Emotion stung at the back of her throat. 'I

think you might've got that the wrong way round.'

His forehead furrowed. 'No. I'm pretty sure it's me who needs to apologise for leaving you at the ball.'

She shook her head. 'And I'm relatively certain I know the reason why that happened.'

She heard an uncomfortable cough come from the three kings' corner of the stable. *Charles.*

He stepped forward. 'Perhaps you two would like some privacy?'

None of the villagers moved. Esme couldn't help it. She laughed. A real-life Christmas drama! She looked at Max whose face read pretty easily. Yes. Some privacy might be nice. Esme searched out one of the publicans from amongst the crowd. 'All right if we nip inside by the fire for a wee bit?'

He nodded and a path was cleared.

Once inside the pub Esme pulled one of Max's big strong hands into hers. 'I thought you had just left. I was terrified I'd never see you again.'

Max's features softened. 'That was definitely one of the plans.'

278 MAKING CHRISTMAS SPECIAL AGAIN

'One of…?'

He tilred his head from side to side. 'I had a few.'

Esme's chest tightened. *Please, please, please, let one of his plans be with her.*

'The one I like best involves a lot of travel.'

Her hands flew to her mouth to stem a host of follow-up questions.

'I went to the Clyde this afternoon and asked them if I could split my shifts between there and the hospital up the road from Heatherglen. I thought… I *hoped* you might be interested in seeing what we had between us might bring if we saw each other a bit more regularly.'

Her heart skipped a beat. 'What are you saying?'

'I'm saying I love you, Esme. I don't want to stop seeing you. One night away from you with all that insecurity and fear tearing at my heart and…' He folded his hands over his heart. 'I don't want to live like that. I'm prepared to fight your brother for your honour if need be.'

'Luckily that won't be necessary,' Esme

assured him, the smile on her face nearly stretching from ear to ear.

'You're the one I'm meant to be with. I will do everything in my power to convince you that I'm the man for you if you'll have me.' He went down on one knee, holding both of her hands in his. 'You are my heart, my soul and everything I could have imagined that would make me a better man. Please say you'll give me a second chance.'

A different kind of tears welled in her eyes. Christmas was meant to be a time of giving. Of opening up one's heart to those you loved, and she loved Max. She'd let fear and her complicated past override what she knew to be true. That she and Max loved each other. She'd fled that ball like a frightened girl. She was a woman now. It was time to start acting like one. She leant forward and kissed Max with every ounce of passion she could muster.

When they started hearing applause coming from the pub windows they both laughed. 'Looks like privacy is hard to come by here in Cluchlochry!' Max waved at the crowd, who cheered.

'Would you like to come back to Heatherglen for some hot chocolate? I think we probably need to talk a bit more.'

Relief flooded Max's features. 'I'd like nothing more.'

When he rose and pulled her into his arms for another soft kiss, a chorus of 'Ahh…' and a second round of applause cocooned them in the village's heartfelt delight. This, Esme thought as she pressed her hand to Max's chest to feel the cadence of his heartbeat, was where she belonged. With this man who would love her and stand by her side through thick and thin. 'What a way to turn round one of the worst Christmas Eves ever,' she whispered.

'Just wait until you see what I have in store for Christmas morning,' he whispered back in a voice that left little to the imagination.

She slipped her mittened hand into his, rested her head against his shoulder and smiled. Christmas was back exactly to where she'd been hoping to find it. In her heart. She looked up at the sky and sent a special prayer to her family who were no longer with them, knowing that they would be over the moon for her. Letting go of the grief she'd carried all these years would take time but filling that void with love was the very best Christmas gift of all.

After three mugs of hot chocolate and hours of heartfelt conversation, Esme and Max were agreed. Honesty was not only the best policy; it was the *only* policy. Charles had generously volunteered to look after Dougal and Wylie for the night, but when Max and Esme awoke on Christmas morning, Esme sneaked into her brother's room to take them into the sitting room for a yuletide cuddle.

'I think Dougal looks good as a reindeer,' Esme insisted as she adjusted the antlers headband she'd perched on top of his little puppy head.

'I think Dougal will do anything to bring a smile to your face.' Max pulled her close to him and gave her a kiss. 'Which makes two of us.'

'Good!' Esme clapped her hands and pulled out a present from behind her back. 'Now it's your turn.'

Max opened the present and let out a huge laugh. 'Seriously? This is what you want me to wear?' He held up the jumper. It was probably the most awful Christmas jumper he'd ever seen in his life. Pom-poms. Blinking reindeer nose. Sequins. Everything that would normally send him running for the hills.

'I had it made specially.' Esme fluttered her eyelashes. 'You wouldn't want to make me sad by not wearing it, would you?'

Max laughed. 'Of course not, darlin'.' He pulled it on and held out his arms. 'Look good?'

Esme nodded. 'Perfect.' She pulled another package from under the tree.

'What's that?'

She giggled. 'One for me! I knew Charles would never buy one so I got one for all of us.'

'You goof.'

'I know, I just… I love Christmas so much and after years of trying to pretend I was having a brilliant time, it finally it feels right.'

'I hope that's because you are precisely where you belong.' Max pulled her to him and gave her a deep kiss. 'With me.'

'Exactly.' Esme grinned. 'Now…' She unfurled her own jumper. 'What do you think of this?'

'You've never looked more beautiful.' Max said dryly.

'And you've never looked more handsome,' she quipped. 'Shall we take a look in the mirror?'

When they went over to the large gilt mirror hanging above the fireplace they both started giggling. 'We look ridiculous,' Esme said, barely able to control herself. 'Ridiculous and perfect.'

Max frowned at their reflection. 'There's something missing.'

'What?' Esme shot him a panicked look. 'You don't have any more secrets up your sleeve, do you?'

Max ruffled her hair and gave her a soft kiss. 'No. I am so sorry about everything that happened at the ball. The best-laid plans and all that. It was stupid of me to want to wait until Christmas Eve to tell you. I made a real hash of things, didn't I?'

'Nothing you didn't fix.' Esme gave his hands a reassuring squeeze. 'Nothing you can't spend the rest of your days making up for,' she said in a much saucier voice.

'In which case...perhaps you'd like to hear my proposal?'

Her cheeks instantly went pink. 'Oh, Max, I love you so much, but you know how I feel about that.'

'I do,' he said, popping a kiss on his finger then transferring it to her nose. 'And I respect it. Which is why I was thinking we might do something a little different.'

'What kind of different?' She might not want to dive into a white frock anytime soon, but that certainly didn't mean she wanted to try anything too off piste. She was, after all, a traditional romantic at heart.

'This kind of different.' He held up his pinkie finger and crooked it. 'I want to be your pinkie promise forever man.'

She giggled. 'Is that even a thing?'

'It is if we make it a thing.'

She stilled when she realised he was absolutely serious. 'What do we have to say?'

He shrugged. 'Nothing formal like wedding vows... Shall I go first?'

She nodded, too choked up with emotion to say anything back.

He crooked his pinkie with hers, looked straight into her eyes and said, 'Esme Ross-Wylde, I love you. You make the world a better place to live in. And one day I'd like to live in it with you by my side.'

'One day?'

He laughed softly. 'All the days if I'm being completely honest, but… I want to make sure what we have makes you the happiest woman on earth.'

'It does.' It was out before she could stop it.

'Good.' Max dipped his head to kiss her, his lips brushing against hers as he finished. 'Then let's take our time. Because all of mine is all of yours. Happy Christmas, love.'

'Best. Christmas. Ever.'

They sealed the promise with a kiss, knowing in each of their hearts that Christmas would for evermore be the happiest, most blessed day of the year.

CHAPTER TWELVE

Two years later

'I CAN'T BELIEVE it's snowing!'

'I can!' Margaret laughed. 'Everything you've wished for since you and Max got engaged has come true. It's like that engagement ring of yours came with magical powers.'

'Only the magical power of love,' Esme teased. She held up the beautiful seasonal bouquet the florist had crafted for her. It was a bountiful mix of heather, holly berries and scarlet roses, dappled with fronds of spruce with miniature pinecones as seasonal flourishes. 'Are you going to be the one to catch this?'

Margaret laughed. 'You can count on it.'

There was a knock on the door. Charles came in when Esme had made sure it wasn't Max trying to get a sneak peek at the bride.

'How's my wee sister doing on her wedding day?'

'Amazing.' She smiled up at him then across to the pictures of her father and Nick. 'I wish they could be here.'

'They are.' Charles gave her a warm smile then pointed to his heart then her own. 'They're here with us.'

'I still can't believe Mum came home.'

'I know! Yet another Christmas miracle!' He laughed and crooked his arm. 'Ready to go and meet your groom?'

'More than ever.'

When Esme came through the small chapel doors and into the cosy church festooned with garlands, Max could hardly breathe. Two years together and she still took his breath away.

Behind her, bearing the rings, were Dougal and Wylie. Behind them were Margaret and a string of bridesmaids dressed in deep evergreen-coloured dresses. But he only had eyes for Esme. Her eyes glittered with anticipation as she walked past the packed congregation towards the altar. There'd be even more people at the reception. Testament to the respect Esme had garnered in her community and beyond. He could not have been more proud of her than he was at this moment.

When Charles handed Esme's hand to him with a stern but loving reminder to take care of his sister, Max answered solemnly. 'I will take care of her until the end of time.'

Esme gave his hand a squeeze and smiled up at him. 'Are you ready for this?'

'More than ever.'

'Do you think they'll let us skip ahead to the kissing the bride bit?' he whispered.

'Don't you worry.' Esme's smile grew. 'We've got a lifetime of kissing ahead of us.'

'In that case…' Max and Esme turned to the minister and nodded. They were ready, hand in hand, to embark on the rest of their lives together, taking a special handful of Christmas magic along with them as they went.

* * * * *

'How's my wee sister doing on her wedding day?'

'Amazing.' She smiled up at him then across to the pictures of her father and Nick. 'I wish they could be here.'

'They are.' Charles gave her a warm smile then pointed to his heart then her own. 'They're here with us.'

'I still can't believe Mum came home.'

'I know! Yet another Christmas miracle!' He laughed and crooked his arm. 'Ready to go and meet your groom?'

'More than ever.'

When Esme came through the small chapel doors and into the cosy church festooned with garlands, Max could hardly breathe. Two years together and she still took his breath away.

Behind her, bearing the rings, were Dougal and Wylie. Behind them were Margaret and a string of bridesmaids dressed in deep evergreen-coloured dresses. But he only had eyes for Esme. Her eyes glittered with anticipation as she walked past the packed congregation towards the altar. There'd be even more people at the reception. Testament to the respect Esme had garnered in her community and beyond. He could not have been more proud of her than he was at this moment.

When Charles handed Esme's hand to him with a stern but loving reminder to take care of his sister, Max answered solemnly. 'I will take care of her until the end of time.'

Esme gave his hand a squeeze and smiled up at him. 'Are you ready for this?'

'More than ever.'

'Do you think they'll let us skip ahead to the kissing the bride bit?' he whispered.

'Don't you worry.' Esme's smile grew. 'We've got a lifetime of kissing ahead of us.'

'In that case…' Max and Esme turned to the minister and nodded. They were ready, hand in hand, to embark on the rest of their lives together, taking a special handful of Christmas magic along with them as they went.

* * * * *